FULL HOUSE

FULL HOUSE

stories by WENDY FAIREY

SOUTHERN METHODIST
UNIVERSITY PRESS
Dallas

This collection of stories is a work of fiction.
Names, characters, places, and incidents are either the product
of the author's imagination or are used fictitiously.

Requests for permission to reproduce material
from this work should be sent to:
Southern Methodist University Press
PO Box 750415
Dallas, Texas 75275-0415

Full House contains several stories published previously in slightly different form. "Over the Hill" appeared in *Season of Adventure: Traveling Tales and Outdoor Journeys of Women over 50,* edited by Jean Gould, Seattle: Seal Press, 1996; and "Her Hair" in *Dutiful Daughters: Caring for Our Parents as They Grow Old,* edited by Jean Gould, Seattle: Seal Press, 1999. "Mind and Body" was included in *A Woman Like That: Lesbian and Bisexual Writers Tell Their Coming Out Stories,* edited by Joan Larkin, New York: Avon Books, 1999. "Grace" appeared in *13th Moon: A Feminist Literary Magazine* XV/1 and 2 (1997).

Cover art: "Reine de Trèfle" by Nelson Blanco
Jacket and text design by Kellye Sanford

Library of Congress Cataloging-in-Publication Data

Fairey, Wendy W.
    Full house : stories / by Wendy Fairey.— 1st ed.
        p. cm.
    ISBN 0-87074-483-6 (acid-free paper)
    1. Women college teachers—Fiction. 2. East Hampton (N.Y.)—Fiction.
    3. Middle aged women—Fiction. 4. New York (N.Y.)—Fiction. 5. Single
    mothers—Fiction. 6. Bisexual women—Fiction. I. Title.

PS3606.A375F85 2003
813'—dc22
                                                                    2003057336

Printed in the United States of America on acid-free paper
10   9   8   7   6   5   4   3   2   1

In memory of Anna Cancogni

ACKNOWLEDGMENTS

I thank the participants of the East End Writers' Group, who helped me realize the potential for a book of stories and offered their astute guidance as I brought the project to completion: Dolores Klaich, Joe Kennedy, Ruth Jacobsen, Marilyn Mehr, Joan Powers, and Jonathan Silin.

With special note of our stimulating exchanges and her encouragement, I thank my friend Sandra Robinson. For their support of friendship and always insightful attention to my work, I thank Joan Larkin, Joanna Torrey, Roni Natov, Ellen Tremper, Rachel Brownstein, Jeanne Betancourt, John Major, who also introduced me to Southern Methodist University Press, Jean Gould, who worked with me in editing her anthologies, and Robert Lescher, whose backing was crucial. I am grateful to my extraordinarily attentive editor, Kathryn M. Lang, of SMU Press, as well as to copyeditor

Robin Whitaker and production and marketing manager George Ann Goodwin.

I have benefited from the support of the PSC-CUNY Research Fund, which awarded me a Creative Incentive Award, and from the general encouragement of creative endeavor on the part of my employer, Brooklyn College.

Finally, I wish to thank my children and grandchildren: Emily, Sean, Louise, Samuel, Zoé, and Gaspard. Their presence in my life has shaped the vision that informs this work.

Nel mezzo del cammin di nostra vita
Mi retrovai per una silva oscura
Che la diritta via era smaritta
DANTE

In the middle of life's path
I found myself in a dark forest
Where the straight way was lost.

CONTENTS

$\mathcal{M}$ENOPAUSE AND $\mathcal{P}$OKER

$\mathcal{A}$t our monthly women's poker game we are talking about menopause.

"I'm telling everyone," says Miriam, "that I went on vacation to Alaska in order to cool down from my hot flashes."

Miriam has just returned from a two-week cruise in the Bering Straits with her husband, Neil. From the ship's observation deck she saw hundreds of sleek brown seals floating by on glistening white ice floes. Menopause, however, did not abate. "One of my flashes," she says, gesturing with both hands to open wide an imaginary trench coat, "could have melted an iceberg."

"How do you know if you're in menopause?" asks Janice, with a quick toss of her silky, long blond hair. She turns to face Miriam to her right at the table.

Janice, who laughs easily at others' jokes and says little

about herself, is the only member of our group under forty. She has yet to have a winning night at cards. "Lucky in love," I almost hazard, but restrain myself in case she's not.

"If you have to ask," replies Miriam, "you're not in it. You'll know." Miriam seems proud to be our vanguard into a region where the rest of us, aside from Janice, will soon be groping our way. The lilt in her voice is accompanied by a visionary gleam in her dark brown eyes. She speaks as an initiate, a priestess, a sibyl, and helps herself to another serving of tofu.

Our evenings always begin with a light supper. Bitsy, the best cook among us, has made the delicately spiced tofu for us—her exotic culinary range must have developed from all those years of fieldwork in Tanzanian and Papuan villages. Janice has brought the assortment of apples, pears, and cherries; Leslie a string bean salad; Vivyan the wine. Miriam has provided the loaves of bread and the soft drinks. I, not a cook since the domestic early days of my marriage when I undertook to prepare a dish out of Julia Child every night, have opted, as usual, to buy the cheese.

Miriam wants to start a menopause support group. Its members will wear T-shirts with HOT FLASHERS in big block letters across the front and, on the back, A PAUSE IS NOT A PERIOD.

"Great!" proclaims Leslie, author of a sweeping sociological study of women's work and play, from prehistory to the present. She sits wearing one of her many T-shirts that have logos about women getting the last word.

I feel as I did in sixth grade when a bunch of us clustered in the girls' bathroom at morning recess to inspect Angela Davenport's size 32B brassiere. We were all eleven, but Angela, big for her age with a figure midway between voluptuous and beefy, had advanced precociously in the mysterious set of changes called DEVELOPMENT. Certainly she was far ahead of me. I had felt my own breasts stirring and growing, pushing out from my flat skinny chest with the force of a tooth coming through the gum or a tender young plant shoot breaking through the surface of the earth. But dramatic to me as their arrival seemed, they were still a private delectation. In the world of sixth-grade pubescence, they were unheralded, unassuming little objects.

I remember the startling roundness of Angela Davenport's breasts, encased in, constrained by the white brassiere. Can it still be called "development" nearly forty years later, when the hormones that stirred and reshaped our young bodies finally slow down and then pack up, calling it a day?

Miriam is now telling us a story about an Alaskan bear that dined on an unfortunate traveler's brain. I sit in my usual seat at one end of the large rectangular table, flanked by Miriam in her habitual seat to my right and Vivyan to my left. Vivyan, at forty-seven, still a self-proclaimed "baby"—though what self-indulgence she excuses by this isn't quite clear—has finished eating. With her elbows propped on the table and her chin resting on her flexible-wristed, long-boned hands, she listens to Miriam. I marvel at Vivyan's hands. They are at once languorous and intensely nervous.

If a bear seems to notice you, Miriam says, you mustn't run. First stand facing it. Try to talk to it. Gesture. Show that you are human. Then, if it charges, hunker down in a fetal position and do your best to protect your head and genitals. Such were the videotaped instructions Miriam received before venturing into the Alaskan wild.

Lost in the middle of a dark forest. Dante's *silva oscura* blurs in my mind with imagined scenes of Alaskan pine forests, tracked by moose and bears padding through a grid of dusky light and deep shadows. The middle of anything— a dark forest, a voyage, a life—seems a difficult place to be.

Miriam is beautiful—she has a vivid dark radiance—and she is heavy. I find the heaviness a part of her beauty. Greeting you at the door of her Jane Street loft, she draws you in to warm capacious hugs. There she is, benign, indisputable, reassuring. It's daunting, however, to think of so much flesh in a state of thermal disequilibrium. A hot flash for Miriam seems a very different order of magnitude from what it would be for me.

When I said as much recently to my medically knowledgeable friend Wanda (Wanda came to poker only once, but more about that later), she explained to me that heavy women tend to have an easier time with menopause because their fat cells continue to produce estrogen. Wanda vows she will never have estrogen replacement therapy, even though it lessens the danger of heart failure. Wanda insists she doesn't fear dying of a heart attack, but she *is* afraid of dying of cancer, which has been linked with estrogen imbalance. Wanda also says that women who have given birth to children—she and I each have had two—can expect, even if we're not heavy, to have less severe menopausal symptoms.

I am a small to average-sized woman—not tall and reasonably thin. Or rather, people often see me as thin, but it's really that I'm compact. I like my body, even to the point of some vanity. I particularly like the more supple upper half. My breasts turned out all right, not too big, not too small. They even drew a compliment from my nice female gynecologist, Dr. Theresa Luponi, when I went for my last annual checkup. My nipples, she said enthusiastically, still projected forward, whereas hers . . . Here her expression grew wistful as she gestured with her two index fingers toward the ground.

Another point of pride with me is that I'm an athlete. I've always played tennis, biked, and swum and hiked, but now that I'm in my late forties, these exertions become more deliberate. Much of the time I feel sore. My feet ache; my knees are stiff; I have twinges of bursitis in my elbow. But I can still get beyond the aches and pains to something I cautiously call transcendence: the moment when limits stretch, almost melt away, and the body, so extended into motion, no longer exists as a contained, containing object. It has become imagination.

Tonight I have cycled to poker on my new touring bike. I rode the four miles from my neighborhood of well-tended

Brooklyn brownstones, passing through slums and the downtown area on the Brooklyn side, then over the arching path of the famous bridge as I pedaled into the deepening blue of early evening, swerving to give way to Brooklyn-bound pedestrians and bikers, finally into Manhattan, onto Chambers Street, then Hudson, threading my way among the slow-moving cars of the evening rush hour. The cheese bounced in my backpack as I crossed over the creases and fissures in the road. The weather was hot, and I worried about melting Brie and sweating Jarlsburg, but there was a heady freedom in moving along outdoors. In my inner sense of myself, I am still a ten-year-old tomboy, androgynous and untrammeled. I haven't minded being a woman, gestating and lactating. And even menstruation with its pains and inconveniences hasn't truly bothered me. Still, there will be a welcome release in being done with it all.

The question, of course, is done with what. Childbearing? I haven't had a baby in twenty years. Sex? Perhaps. Desire? That would be something, not to feel desire, not to have to contend with it. As far back as my hopeless schoolgirl crushes on teachers and popular girls, I have felt confused about whom to want, what to want. And *being* wanted hasn't been easy for me either, turned too readily into pressure and responsibility. I marvel at the unabashed boldness of others, how Leslie, for example, can boast about sexual exploits or recount with such glee how a few years back she placed an ad in the *Village Voice*—"classy female sociologist seeks . . . ," to which she got four hundred responses. Or how Vivyan, in her cool, understated way, can drop little asides about the world showering her with compliments. Recently the group was having a conversation about looking or not looking our age, and Vivyan slipped in the fact that a doorman had told her, "You're the most elegant woman I've seen all week." I don't know if the others at the poker table heard her. They made no comment.

I happen to agree with the doorman. Tall and thin with those long expressive hands, Vivyan has a style I admire. I like the way she can dismiss her former lover Michael with a terse flick of the wrist. "Ah Michael," she says as the hand completes its loop. And that's it for Michael—consigned to drab, joyless domesticity with his young new wife and infant. Still, I couldn't think what to say about the door-man's compliment. A week seemed a strange unit of time for him to fix on. Why not a day? A month? A lifetime?

And what if I am almost done with youthfulness? If we all are? Will the doorman compliment Vivyan ten years from now? Or twenty? Will Leslie still have her exploits? I don't look forward to withering or watching age assault my friends. But riding my bicycle this blue-toned evening, I elude the consciousness of time. Accelerating my rotation of the pedals, I feel like Hermes. I'm a shaft of muscle and movement, not a mother, a divorcée, a professional, not an earthbound, flesh-encumbered, middle-aged woman on the climacteric brink.

The poker game was Miriam's inspiration. "I want to play poker," she said to me and our mutual good friend Leslie, as the three of us, about a year and a half ago, gathered for one of our dinners at Whole Wheat and Wild Berries, Miriam's favorite vegetarian restaurant.

"What a great idea," said Leslie, whose certitude always cuts off room for others' doubts.

"Yes," I echoed, hiding my weaker conviction. I hadn't liked fish or canasta, and they were the only card games I knew, aside from a game called AUTHORS, the object of which, as far as I could remember, was to corner a set of four bearded Henry Wadsworth Longfellows or Charles Dickenses or the same number of mustachioed Nathaniel Hawthornes or Edgar Allan Poes. In college I had resisted the lure of bridge—it seemed a pernicious temptation to idleness. Once I had played blackjack and once roulette. But I didn't like gambling. It unsettled me. I felt too keenly the stakes.

"Why poker?" I asked Miriam. "Do *you* know how to play poker?"

"No," she said earnestly. "I want to *learn*. That's the point. I want to learn to take calculated risks."

Miriam had risked her own money and what she could raise from backers to start a nightclub in the seventies, then spent the eighties digging herself out of debt. I hadn't known her then, though in an odd way we went way back. In 1960, the year we were both seventeen, we had, quite unknown to one another, shared a boyfriend—tall, taciturn, twenty-three-year-old David Whitman. Miriam had slept with him; I, no less memorably, had spent an hour with him on a couch, engaged in the first prone kissing of my life. That hour stood enshrined as my first experience of sexual pleasure and my second of any sex play at all. Three years earlier, on the way home from our date at the movies, a ninth-grade classmate had French-kissed me in the back seat of his family car, while his grandmother, our front-seat chaperon and chauffeur, kept her eyes riveted on the road. The next day, tremulous with disgust, I had removed the dog tag slipped around my neck in the discreet dark of the theater and thrown it into the street. With gloomy satisfaction I had watched the passing cars run over it. I had not then kissed another boy until David Whitman, though he, I guess, could be called a man. That was part of his appeal.

David had been in the army and was putting himself through college. Miriam told me he had been a real bastard. I don't remember what I had thought of his character. I do remember the eagerness tinged with shame with which, ostensibly to check out books, I had gone out of my way to the branch of the public library where he worked. "Ah, fancy meeting you here." Finally—but before the evening on the couch—I had mustered the courage to invite him to my boarding school prom. He had accepted, and I remember the feel of my ear pressed against the third stud of his dress shirt as we danced to the music of Lester Lanin. Meanwhile,

Miriam had slept with him and then married Neil, who was David's younger brother. I heard from Miriam that David has had a disappointing life.

There were to be no men at the poker game. It wasn't necessary to discuss including them or to explain the reasons for keeping them out. The plan was simply to get a group of friends, women friends, together, and Miriam offered to have the games at her loft.

"What about Neil?" asked Leslie.

"Oh, don't worry about him," said Miriam. "He won't be there." I tried to imagine the conversation in which Neil, no longer the willowy, delicate-featured youth I had glimpsed in 1960, but portly, balding, middle-aged, was given notice of his monthly exile. Other people's marriages were mysteriously resonant with the intimacy of their accommodations.

The original group of women who met in Miriam's loft included a dark-haired Frenchwoman named Chantal—Miriam said she was a great photographer—who had played a lot of poker in Paris. She taught us that a flush in French is *couleur*, but then dropped out because poker reminded her of her drinking days and she wanted to stay on the wagon.

We also lost Leslie's friend Nan, a professional administrator in city government. It was Nan who explained how to play five-card draw and seven-card stud and who taught us to use two decks of cards, so that one would always be shuffled and ready for the dealer. We were grateful for her organizing influence, but she went too far. Back from a weekend with her card-playing mother, she wanted to change our admittedly irregular formula of "winner-take-all." We liked it that one person could win twenty-five or thirty dollars and no one would lose more than the five each of us put into the pot. "Let's just try it the right way," said Nan. Politely we went along with her, each buying our pile of nickel, dime, and quarter chips, then counting up what we were worth at the end. We felt out of sorts all evening, then vindicated in our resistance when the biggest winner got a paltry $1.75. Nan scolded us for telling jokes during play and spoke sharply to Miriam for not knowing and, worse still, not seeming to care that her hand of four of a kind beat a full house.

The following month Nan was gone. We went back to winner-take-all but upped the ante to seven dollars a player. Miriam handed out copies of a crib sheet. With bullets to accentuate the items, it listed in a large bold font the order of value of the hands, from two of a kind right through to royal flush. Miriam also announced that she had had a revelation. "I've figured something out," she said. "The point of this game is to *win*."

"What else could be the point?" I asked.

"Ah," Leslie exclaimed, ebullient and knowing.

That evening Miriam acted on her insight. Bluffing, pushing up the bets, she scared off the cautious and won the thirty-five dollar pot.

There were other players besides Nan who didn't work

out. One was my friend Gail, who had made the definitive pronouncement on dating: "Of course, dating is awful. The whole agenda's the relationship, and there *is* no relationship." Gail joined us one evening but didn't like poker and played without joy. At the end of the evening when we set the next month's game, though she duly wrote the date in her engagement book, it was clear to her and to us that she wouldn't be back.

"It's a pity," said Leslie, no less appreciative than I of the exquisite black bean casserole Gail had contributed to the dinner. It was from a recipe in *Gourmet* magazine.

"Why be playing a silly game," Gail mused later to me, "when you have so many interesting women in the same room?"

"But the game's the whole point," I explained. "You've got to like the game."

By now, *I* did, to my surprise, as much as anyone. I liked the endurance and persistence, the gaiety in playing, win or lose. It was I, I noticed, who would move us on from eating to handing out the chips or be the one gently to urge, "Let's play poker," if ever play flagged too long in talk of men or mothers or movies—our habitual topics of conversation. I have always been eager to get on with it, whatever "it" is, as if there were really something to get on to. I just like to keep striving at the task at hand and grow impatient with detours and deflections.

My good friend Wanda also came to poker only one time.

We played three practice hands before she began to get the hang of five-card draw, and she floundered anew when we moved on to seven-card high-low, protesting all the while that she didn't like games and was "just not competitive." Then too, Wanda was allergic to cats, so Miriam's much pampered Siamese, Sashimi, had to spend the evening in the bathroom.

"I don't really like her," Leslie said in a loud whisper when Wanda went into the bathroom from which Sashimi had been temporarily liberated. I shrugged evasively and felt torn between loyalties. Leslie had criticized my friend, but, after all, Wanda had invited the criticism. Wanda had got out her date book with the rest of us at the end of the evening. Later, when I heard from Leslie that the date had been changed, I called Wanda to let her know, only then to learn from Miriam that the date had been changed precisely to get rid of Wanda.

"Look," she said, "we're professional women with a lot of responsibilities and obligations. Poker is something we do entirely for fun. We don't have to put up with anyone or anything we don't like." I knew Leslie's was the objecting voice. I wondered if Miriam felt, as I did, slightly afraid of her.

"This is like sixth grade," I complained. That year of burgeoning breasts, I had been a founding member of our very own "Four Musketeers." Its membership of giggling, cookie-baking schoolgirls had quickly swelled to ten, as our chief activity became inviting in and then expelling our classmates. I had gone along with the expulsions—that was one way not to get expelled oneself—but never without guilt or regret.

With the same mix of emotions, I prepared to speak with Wanda. "Do guests necessarily come back?" she asked, making my task blessedly easy.

"No they don't," candor moved me to say. "And I guess I've had my turn at bringing one."

Miriam brought in Bitsy and Janice, who fit right in, and I brought in my Swedish journalist friend, Vivyan. Bitsy was another novice, but a willing learner and a great cook. Janice and Vivyan were experienced players. I had thought of Vivyan because I knew she used to play with her lover Michael.

It was Janice who taught us anaconda. Dealt seven cards down, you look them over and then must pass, successively, three cards, two cards, and one card to your left—passing each time before you pick up what the person to your right has passed to you. The poignancy of anaconda lies in this necessity of discarding from your own hand before you see what your neighbor has given you. Then too, in giving up the first three cards, you may have to break up a hand you hate to part with. You can also play anaconda passing to the right. "ANACONDA . . . TO THE RIGHT!" the dealer calls. The exhilaration of changing directions seemed to me like that of a square dance—*Swing your partner to your left. Allemande right and do-si-do . . .*

Vivyan taught us about wild cards. "Let's play seven-card stud, deuces wild and rolling," she announced the first evening she was with us, with a quiet smile. There was something dangerous and wonderful about the phrase "wild and rolling." We felt a heightened pitch of excitement, for me even greater than that of anaconda.

"But there's got to be a feminist word for *stud*," said Leslie. Janice suggested *bimbo,* but we decided that *stud* had historical legitimacy.

Vivyan posed a small problem, though only at first. She kept putting her chip into the pot before her turn, and Leslie across the table from her kept saying, "Vivyan, it's Bitsy's turn, not yours."

"I like Vivyan, but I don't love her," Leslie said to me at the end of the evening.

"Oh, I like her a lot," I countered. Meanwhile, Vivyan told me that though she had liked Bitsy as a person, she couldn't stand the slow pace of her play. The following month I abandoned what I had come to regard as my lucky seat at the head of the table—I had sat in it the two times I had won—to take the chair next to Bitsy so that Leslie wouldn't have occasion to reprimand Vivyan. Vivyan won, coolly outstripping me on the last hand, a round of five-card draw, pair of jacks or better to start.

"But what if no one has jacks or better?" Janice had inquired at the start of the round.

"You get new cards and have to ante anew," Vivyan had

knowingly explained. "But then it's queens or better to start. And the next time kings. And so on."

Three busted hands had swelled the pot. Finally I could play two aces, but Vivyan had topped me with three sixes. When we counted our chips for the evening, hers was the largest pile.

Winner-take-all.

"I hated to beat *you*, Jenny," said Vivyan.

And Miriam said, "I think we have our group."

FAMILY PETS

Sashimi presses against my right leg, which I have curled around the back of my chair at the poker table. His body vibrates with pleasure. I expect him to move on, to glide toward the feet of another player or go curl up in a corner of the room. Insistently he lingers, rubbing against my leg in a rhythmic motion. The vibration of his purring penetrates the fabric of my jeans. I consider reaching down to pat his sleek fur, white with a tint of gray. Instead, I disentangle my foot from the chair leg and use it to push him gently away from me. You could say that I give him a discreet little shove. We are still eating our pregame dinner, and I don't want to mix cat hair with my tofu.

"Come to Mama," says Miriam in the seat next to me. "Sashimi-weemi, come to Mama." She reaches with both hands under the table, lifts the cat so that its nose presses against her own, and then settles it into her ample lap. One of her hands caresses its back as she raises the last forkful of beet and goat-cheese salad to her mouth.

"It's uncanny," she says to me. "They always find the person who doesn't like animals."

"No, no," I sputter in vague protest. I don't want to be branded the curmudgeon of my poker group. For good measure, I flash a guilty, disingenuous smile in Sashimi's direction. The cat peers at me inscrutably, then blinks. I return to the last morsels of food on my plate. "I loved my pets when I was a child," I tell Miriam and whomever else at the table might care to know this. Miriam smiles politely, and no one else responds. Janice is clearing plates, Bitsy is rinsing and placing them in the dishwasher. Leslie, in another part of the room, is counting out the chips for that night's game.

2

There's no point in telling the group about my dog Tony. The wounds and poignancies of childhood aren't poker talk, and I try to play by the rules. I guess I might try to toss off as a light aside that my dog was my first great love. But as I think how to say this, to strike just the right tone, the impulse passes.

When Tony died, I was about to turn seventeen, and in an important sense my childhood ended. My mother conveyed the tragic news as she and I sat dining in the Raleigh Room of the Warwick Hotel on Sixth Avenue and Fifty-fourth Street.

Peter, my younger brother, was there too, though he's not at the forefront of my memory of the occasion. The three of us had just returned to the U.S. on the *Queen Mary,* and we were treating ourselves to a few nights at a luxury hotel before moving into our new house in Westport, Connecticut. On the transatlantic crossing, Peter and I had played shuffleboard and bingo, and I had been the runner up in the ladies' ping pong tournament. Earlier, on our holiday in Venice, I had ventured to talk with a real Beat poet I met one day on the beach and to flirt with Count Paolo Carozzi, the twenty-four-year-old eldest son of a family of impoverished aristocrats. Paolo's family had a Tiepolo in the ceiling of their palazzo.

"Would you like to see Venetian nightlife?" he had asked me as we sat beneath the Tiepolo.

"Mommy," I had called across the room to my mother, who was displaying her customary animation and charm in a conversation with the count, Paolo's father, "Can I go see Venetian nightlife?"

It had remained in truth unclear whether Paolo's warmest interest was in me or in my glamorous mother. I had been content to take what came my way, to sip my oran-giata sitting on a stool in Harry's Bar and walk with Paolo arm in arm through narrow streets and over bridges. On one of those bridges he kissed me on the cheek. Later, in Connecticut, I would lie on my bed in my little room with the dormer window, blowing on a hand-painted porcelain whistle of a blue-coated Venetian soldier astride his saddle.

Paolo had brought me this memento of our time together when he came to our hotel to say good-bye to us.

Now, though, I wanted to be reunited with my dog. Since we were in transition between California and the East, it had seemed sensible to leave Tony behind with our friends in the Ojai Valley until we were ready to receive him into our new home. Ojai was one of the spots near Los Angeles where my mother used to take us for getaway weekends. Its natural scenic beauty had been enhanced for her by the attentions of the handsome cowboy who ran the stables at the Ojai Valley Inn and with whom she had a passing affair. The cowboy—who from his brown, wavy hair to his scuffed, studded boots looked the part of Curly in *Oklahoma!*—harbored ambitions to be an actor and thought my film-world mother could help him. Unfortunately, he shattered his nose in a riding accident, and there went his hopes of Hollywood. The horse I used to ride at that stable was called Ginger.

"When is Tony coming East?" I asked my mother.

"There's something I have to tell you," she said. "It's very sad. I hope you can be brave." My mother paused. The pause in itself seemed terrible to me.

"Tony wandered off into the mountains," she said. "He was killed by a mountain lion."

She looked at me intently, trying to gauge the impact of her words. I knew I didn't want to look back at her; the self-exposure would have felt too raw. My eyes stung as I shifted my gaze to the mural spanning the wall nearest our table. At first it was only a blur, but after a while, I couldn't help discerning Sir Walter Raleigh as he knelt in his doublet before Queen Elizabeth. He had spread out his cape on the ground between them so that she could keep her feet dry as she crossed the puddle. My sixteen-year-old life felt as still as the mural. I imagined the mountain lion from his perch on a craggy rock sighting Tony. I imagined him taut and still the moment before leaping.

Only later, as a way to make some sense of what had happened, I thought about Tony's predilection for wandering. He must have gone off on one of his male dog forays, as he used to do at intervals from our home in Beverly Hills. The backyard of our large Spanish-style house was enclosed by a high stucco wall, but there were ways to get out—the iron gates to the driveway, the small wooden service gate to the kitchen, not to mention the back gate to the alley, where we incinerated the trash. Previous dogs, Muffy, the fat cocker spaniel, and Captain, the pedigreed beagle, had dug beneath the kitchen gate and repeatedly escaped. I remember shouting their names up the long, quiet, tree-lined street. What happened to these dogs—Muffy, Captain, and Trixie, the first dog of all, a black medium-sized mongrel? They simply disappeared from our lives, as had the black cat named Jimmy, which turned out to be a female. Muffy left because of the digging; Captain, I think, was considered too high strung. Did we just come home one day and find them gone? I remember their entrance into our lives better than their exits. You might say that pets weren't essential to our household. Or perhaps that we just weren't any good with pets. My mother had been raised in a city orphanage and been too busy making her way in the world to have time and emotion to spare for dependent animals. Of course, she wanted us to have everything privileged children should have, everything *she* hadn't had. So along with our bicycles and tennis lessons and cowboy outfits and trips to Europe, we tried to take on the requisite cat or dog. A few of these, as I recall, were presents from my mother's admirers, who sought to win her through their offerings to her children. We were even given a hamster. But he died when we children forgot to fill his food bin with hamster pellets and replenish his little water bottle. My mother made me as the eldest, and therefore most culpable, carry the rigid carcass out to the incinerator in the back alley. I held it at arm's length by its tail. My mother said this would make me more mindful.

It's not that I didn't adore animals. I devoured every horse and dog book I could find. Black Beauty was my soul mate. Beautiful Joe wrenched my heart in his search for a good home. My friend Flicka moved me to tears as I immersed myself in her ordeals and her heroism. I had read *all* the Black Stallion books—I *was* Alec Ramsey—and the Albert Payson Terhune dog books. I could name every breed of dog and horse and every part of their bodies. It's just that my interest was more literary than practical, more imaginary than applied.

At least until the arrival of Tony.

It always seemed ironic to me that my dog had a human name and my stepfather, who brought Tony into our house, had the nickname of a dog. I was twelve when we got Tony, and he became *my* dog. Giving him to us was the best thing Eddie "Bow Wow" Polaski ever did for me.

Bow Wow had entered our lives two years earlier when he wangled an introduction to my mother and came to see if she might be able to help him raise money for his pet project, "Bow Wow's Boys Town." He brought with him an impressive blueprint, which he spread out on our living room coffee table. BOW WOW'S BOYS TOWN, this said at the top. There were dormitories and classroom buildings and a refectory and playing fields. He told us that his nickname came from the frisky way he used to play college football. I don't know how it happened, but before my mother made her appearance, Bow Wow had turned our living room into a baseball diamond and was throwing a ball to me and my brother, Peter. My mother later said that her first thought as she came down the stairs had been for the furniture. The second had been, "What a wonderful father for the children."

Six weeks later Bow Wow and my mother were married. I never heard anything more about Bow Wow's Boys Town, though the map hung in the office that my mother built for Bow Wow over the garage. He had been persuaded to give up his job as a football coach in a nearby prison and take on what passed for work as my mother's unofficial manager.

She also built him a dressing room off her bedroom. When he moved into our house, he brought in cartons and cartons of old shoes, so I guess he needed that dressing room. My mother and Bow Wow had most of their fights in the bedroom. Mesmerized, Peter and I used to sit on the stairs outside their door and listen to the raised angry voices.

Bow Wow lasted with us three and a half years, during which time he introduced into our home the pigeons, the ducks, the chickens, and Tony. Then he overstepped, though not because of the pets. Rummaging in his office one day when he was out of town, my mother discovered his diary. It had nasty things to say about us all—he opined that I was a brat, Peter a sissy, and our mother a terrible bitch—and it also revealed his schemes to steal our property.

Bow Wow and I were enemies pretty much from the start. I quickly realized he would never be any kind of father to me, and I was always confident I would outlast him. So when our mother gathered us up one weekend and said we were going up to Ojai, and when it turned out she was leaving us there with friends to go home and kick Bow Wow out, I took a steely pleasure in my victory. Still, I have to give Bow Wow his due about the animals.

We had eaten the chickens—though Peter and I were told that these were *our* chickens only after the fact—and got rid of the pigeons and the ducks, banished because our mother said they were too messy, when we came home from school one day to find Tony. From my reading and observation I was partial to collies and golden retrievers and *not* to Dalmatians. But Tony was special. He was a full-grown dog, probably three or four years old, with a largely unspotted white face you would have to call noble and intelligent, framed by heavily spotted, alert ears. His body was long-limbed and supple, and the movement of his strong tail, also almost all white, helped to convey his sensitive engagement with the world around him. Bow Wow told some story about Tony belonging to an actor who was leaving for the East. With Bow Wow you never wanted to inquire into things too closely. We all knew he was a liar. "A pathological liar," said our mother.

Peter and I both fell in love with Tony, though Peter was still too busy playing cowboys and Indians to challenge me as the person who loved Tony best. I kept an old red corduroy cushion for the dog to sleep on at the foot of my bed, and sometimes I would lie on it with him. Nose to nose, I would talk to him about how he was the only one who understood me. I had a crush on a girl in my seventh-grade class. Tony knew all about that; he also knew about my detestation of Bow Wow. More often we would lie together on my bed, and when Tony fell asleep on my legs, I would stay still for what seemed like hours for fear of disturbing him.

One time Bow Wow kicked him. Tony had been discovered in my mother's bedroom chewing one of Bow Wow's shoes. She was present in the room, and so was I. After the kick, I placed myself between Bow Wow and the cowering dog. "You can't do that," I challenged my stepfather. "You can't kick Tony." My mother later said she had been afraid in that moment that Bow Wow would kick *me*. In fact, he never laid a hand on us. That was one of the understood rules of the house.

After my mother got rid of Bow Wow, he tried to get back at us. He called the principal of our school to tell her our mother was a communist, and he sent the ASPCA to our house to investigate mistreatment of a dog. Tony came up to the door wagging his tail.

"Is this a mistreated dog?" asked my mother, with all her flair for righteous indignation.

Despite herself, she too had come to love Tony. The times he escaped from the backyard and would be gone for two or three days, she would ride in our metallic-blue Chrysler station wagon up and down the streets of Beverly Hills calling his name. And when he was hit by a car and brought home bleeding, it was she who rushed him to the vet and asked the doctors to put him together again against all odds. I watched her drive away with him. "It will be all right," she had reassured me, wanting me to trust in her ability to fix things. I had felt afraid; still, I had believed her. And Tony came back to us—at least that time.

"The children had to learn I wasn't God," my mother said in after years. The part of God, though, was a role I think she relinquished with some reluctance.

After his accident, Tony was more sedate. He would lie

with us watching *The $64,000 Question* and other favorite
television shows, only occasionally raising his head to nuz-
zle it in one of our laps. I was worried about him, especially, when the time came for me to leave for boarding school
back East, but my mother and Peter reassured me they
would take good care of him. The plan for me to go away to
school had been formed when Bow Wow was still with us;
my mother said it would be good for me to get away from
the conflicts at home. And who knows? Maybe she thought
my being away would also lessen her conflicts.

Even with Bow Wow gone, the boarding school plan
gained momentum. My mother believed in the power of an
elite education to make my life gentle and gracious in ways
hers had never been. We also agreed that I wasn't your typi-
cal California girl. I was dark-haired and studious, a lover of
history and poetry. The East seemed the place for me to
flower. When we packed my trunk, tucking into its corners
the socks with sewn-on labels, Tony watched from his cushion at the foot of my bed.

3

In my first semester back East, I was the only girl in the
school who made the high honor roll reserved for straight-
A students. Honors were posted in our school Common
Room, and there I encountered my solitary name, set off
from the names of those students with mere honors, which
were grouped lower on the page. Meanwhile, in my dorm

room, my two roommates, Lacey Ellison and Allie Keene, short-sheeted my bed.

I can still feel how my legs jolted against the shortened sheet as I tried to climb into the narrow bed provided by the school—so different, even to begin with, from my nice comfortable bed in my airy room at home. At first, I didn't get the joke, but then, as I did, I turned on Lacey and Allie in humorless fury. They were in their own beds, across the room from mine, looking on, I'm sure, in the hopes of some good fun. "Fix it," I said, scrambling up with as much dignity as I could muster and assuming a sentinel position on the cold stone floor. With barely repressed snickers, they rose and crossed the room. I stood with my arms folded across my nightgown, watching, vigilant and insistent, as they undid their handiwork.

That first term of tenth grade, my mother let me fly to California for the short Thanksgiving break as well as for Christmas. I guess she thought I needed to come home then. I remember a feeling of utter peace and relief the first night back in my own room as I pulled up the fresh bed covers. Tony had greeted me with full tail-wagging excitement, and even Peter seemed pleased to have me home again. Still, at the end of five days, I left without tears, mounting the rolling stairway to the TWA jet bound for New York and waving with good cheer from my window seat as I buckled my seatbelt. At no time then or thereafter did I ask to leave the school.

I did complain in my letters. Especially through the hard

first year, my weekly missives home inventoried my academic triumphs and social defeats, as well as every sore throat and sniffle that beset me. But gradually into this predictable mix crept the alloy of modest social pleasures: the making of a few friends; the account of a nice boy I met at a mixer, who then invited me to *his* school dance as his date; a request to have a classmate visit me in California during the coming summer; my excitement at landing a small part in a play. Sometimes at the end of my letters, I thought to mention Tony, though it would be false to say he was always on my mind. At one point, I went on a campaign to get him mated, so we could have a litter of cute little Dalmatians. Needless to say, nothing came of this.

There were subjects, increasingly, I didn't broach in my letters home. I didn't, for example, write a word to my mother about my epistolary romance with the boy from the mixer. It escalated like a brush fire in the two months between our first meeting and our second, as the letters on both sides grew exponentially more passionate. Then when we met again, we could hardly look at one another, our mutual inhibition was so strong. "If only our lips could have met but once," the boy wrote to me in the aftermath of my visit. "But they didn't," I responded with merciless clarity. "You had your chance." I was scornful of his timidity and saved from having to acknowledge my own. My family life had taught me how to laugh at men. And how to dismiss them.

On a page in my old photo album from those boarding

school years is a snapshot labeled "Last Picture of Tony," taken at Malibu the summer we were to leave California. I flew home right after junior year final exams, and we stayed for a month in a rented beach house before taking off for Europe. Already the Beverly Hills house, my home from the time I was five years old, had been sold. Our new home awaited us in Connecticut, a house purchased in a town only a half-hour drive from my school. Declaring herself fed up with California, my mother was restless. After Bow Wow, something had gone out of her. Peter, too, was starting at an eastern boarding school. She said she wanted to be near her children and to create a new, better life for us all in the East.

In the snapshot, which Peter took on the beach one sunny, breezy afternoon, I am standing with the ocean in the background, holding a coiled rope to which Tony is attached. Dressed in shorts and a sailor-collar shirt, smiling and relaxed, I face the camera. My figure, which a year earlier was still scrawny, has filled out. Tony is turned away from me with his head and body pointing toward the ocean. Although his face is not visible in the photo, every detail of his posture—a raised foreleg, his perky ears and tail, the slightly forward angle of his body—signifies his eagerness to get going. Shortly I'll be running with him along the sand, all the way to the jutting rocks that mark the end of the beach. As we lope along, I will let out the length of rope so that he can enjoy as much freedom as possible. Probably I'll let him off the leash entirely, a liberty my mother opposes for fear of his running off. But I can scurry to keep up with him and then cajole him back to me to grasp his collar and snap on the leash. My mother will never know.

When our Ojai friends come to take Tony away for the rest of the summer, I promise him that he will like his new home in Connecticut, though privately I worry how well he will adapt to cold and snow. Still, it pleases me to think that I will get to see him more often. My mother has said one advantage of the new house will be that I can come home on weekends. If this doesn't strike me as an unmixed blessing, it is only because I am by now less eager to spend time with *her* than I used to be when I was younger.

4

I never had another pet after Tony. Our *vita nuova* in Connecticut never quite jelled. And, in any case, a new pet would have made no sense. Peter and I were both off at school and then college; my mother was never convincing as a homebody—how could a pet have been fit in? Later, during the years I was married to Richard and our children, Sarah and Matthew, were young, the children had pets. But though I helped take care of these with due diligence and even with affection, I never really thought of them as mine.

Unfortunately, our luck with pets was poor, and a number of them met with untimely ends. It was nobody's fault that the German shepherd Francesca had a seizure, or that a ladder was inadvertently dropped on Fluffy, the gray kitten, or that Blackie, the cat I was especially fond of, failed to survive surgery for stomach ulcers. Yet such mishaps only served to reinforce my general wariness of attachment to animals.

Most macabre of all was the demise of the gerbil that Sarah, at four, brought home from her nursery school for a weekend visit. Playing with it in creative ways, she placed it on a movable elevator platform of a Fisher Price toy garage, started cranking this platform up and down, and, alas, broke the gerbil's neck. I discovered this critical state of affairs when I found Sarah in the bathroom, running tap water over the limp carcass trying to revive it. At once, I called Sarah's teacher to make my abject apologies. Naturally, I offered to find a replacement gerbil, but the teacher, with more emphasis than seemed called for, said "no need." I was surprised that she seemed relieved to be rid of the poor creature.

I was worried that little Sarah might be scarred by this experience, and I felt bad about the gerbil. Still, some wall had gone up in my soul to shield me from the sharpest edge of such disasters. I took refuge in irony. I stopped reaching to pet other people's dogs and cats. I cut off, not my liking for animals, but my interest in them. My effort was to stay open to people. That seemed challenge enough.

5

Until very recently, I had always believed my mother's story of Tony and the mountain lion—believed in it, from that wrenching moment in the Raleigh Room onward, without the shadow of a second thought. But as I walked recently with my friend Vivyan, as is our pastime, strolling along Hudson Street one afternoon shortly after our last poker game, the subject arose of family pets.

"You know, I don't dislike animals," I reassured her—and myself. "I loved my dog, but he was killed by a mountain lion."

Vivyan has a way of just raising an eyebrow, and everything is called into question.

"Do you think my mother lied to me?" I stopped on the sidewalk. The enormity of the betrayal presented itself like an abyss I couldn't cross. If Bow Wow, or for that matter any of the men who had come and gone in our lives, had been expendable, Tony wasn't. He belonged to our essential family, and his death had been a family tragedy, mourned, I believed, by us all with the purest grief. Almost at once, I was back in the Raleigh Room. Sir Walter in his doublet knelt before me, spreading his cape for the Virgin Queen. I had always imagined the Queen passing unspotted to the other side of the puddle. Now I saw her sinking in the mud as the cape itself sank beneath her weight. Sir Walter's spreading of the cape had been a futile gesture.

"Well," Vivyan said placing her hand gently on my elbow to urge the resumption of our pace. "I can't answer that. And you? Do you really want to? Some things perhaps aren't meant to be questioned."

GRACE

Of course, Grace Ellen Blau didn't come to our twenty-fifth college reunion. Would she even have wanted to come? Reunions don't seem to draw people with ruined lives. To me it was clear that those who turned up—whatever their frank disclosures of divorces or unfulfilled ambitions, illnesses or serious problems with children—had something to show for themselves, something—as much perhaps spirit as achievement—they wanted to show. Why would anyone come if she didn't? It's true one poor woman, whom I remembered from French 201—*La Chanson de Roland* to La Bruyère—wandered ill with sadness through the three days of picnics and meetings and dinners, a pale, tangibly melancholy, childishly unfocused figure, soft and blurred. But her plight was not permanent madness.

I'm not sure how often Grace even left her apartment.

Once she had called me to ask, in that rasping voice, if it was all right to drive by my house—her parents were planning to take her for a Sunday outing. I saw in my mind's eye a wan, middle-aged face—so I imagined her—peering from a car's rear window, poignantly excited by a brownstone facade, the blank of shutters. Not without a touch of fear, I gave permission, but the excursion fell through. Perhaps Patty, her nurse, took Grace out sometimes to do a few errands or to sit on a park bench on a nice day.

I hadn't told Grace I was planning to attend the reunion. In all the years she had been making her phone calls to me, I never volunteered information. Nor did I ask her questions other than, "Oh hello, Grace. How are you?" Those were my ground rules. To be polite, even friendly, but do nothing to encourage familiarity. To listen for a minute or so, then tell her I had to go.

Once, though, on a whim, I returned her call. She wanted to know my zip code in order to send me a valentine. That was the message I found on my machine. And so I called the number I had never copied into my address book, to give her the code in one measured, matter-of-fact sentence. Later I judged this had been a mistake. Even this scant measure of responsiveness unsettled her. She phoned at least ten times, repeating the code to verify that it wasn't a false message of the mind agents, asking if I minded a smudged envelope, explaining that she was simply too worn out with loneliness to copy the address over one more time. Three separate envelopes arrived, one of them indeed rumpled and greasy, each containing poems and candy kisses. They were the only valentines I got that year.

Grace Ellen Blau was a casualty. She had gone crazy during our junior year. The rumor spread she had tried to jump off Rockefeller Tower. She never came back to graduate, though at the time I'm not sure I noticed. She was a philosophy and I a double English and French major. We had no classes together. I hardly knew her. Still, the first time, nine years back, when she got in touch to warn me that evil forces were trying to steal my thoughts, I remembered her right away, as soon as she said her name. I didn't recognize the voice—how could I have? Whatever it had been, it was altered to that rasp. But without hesitation I knew who she was.

She flashed before me sitting on the wall by her dorm as I walked past—a small tomboyish figure, dressed in jeans, Keds, and a green, loose-fitting V-neck sweater—sitting on the wall with her catlike gray eyes. Her knees were pulled up so she could rest her chin on them. My friend Joanne had told me back then that Grace had a crush on me, and I think I had said, "How can she? She doesn't even know me." I remember wondering if Grace had seen me as Ophelia in our college production of *Hamlet,* but Joanne, as I recall, didn't know. Now, after Grace's first call, I tracked down Joanne in California, as someone who might bring me up to date. The Grace of today, she was able to tell me, chain-smoked and weighed over two hundred pounds. Grace had for a time kept phoning her until Joanne had felt compelled to tell her to stop.

I made clear to Grace in one of our early conversations that I didn't want to hear about conspiracies.

"What do you want to hear about?" she asked.

"Well," I said, "you can tell me what you're reading. That would be very interesting."

She read a great deal. Virginia Woolf. Hemingway. *Being Blue: A Philosophical Inquiry,* by William Gass. That was one of her recommendations. I went out and bought the book. Sometimes the paranoia slipped in.

"I'm reading *War and Peace*," she told me. "But I think they switched copies on me. I keep reading. And there's only war. No peace. No peace."

I guess it had all been sadness and madness since she left college. The messages suggested her history. She said more when she spoke to the machine than when she got me in person. It wasn't just that I encouraged brevity. Even when, as an experiment, I decided to let her be the one to end the conversation, it was telling how quickly she got off. I think she expected not to reach me and felt unsettled and abashed when she did.

To the machine she could be more expansive.

"I was sold into deep mental slavery," she recorded. "I was held a mental captive for twenty-six years. I haven't been able to take a vacation. I'm not eating properly. And Patty Donnally, the nurse, says, 'Oh it's a prison, but you like prison. You fit well here. Here's a piece of steak.'

"But I say, 'I don't want steak. I want my freedom.'

"What America did to me was the most incredible ridiculous nonsense. An M.D. Cohen. Sixty-eighth Street. Doctor M.D. Cohen. She has to be looked into. She has to be researched and tracked and traced. Dr. M. D. Cohen on Sixty-eighth Street and Madison Avenue sold me into utter slavery, total slavery, where I was tortured and tormented, needled at every single point of weakness—acupuncture of the soul. Four thousand points of weakness were stuck into me, knifelike into me, by the media, by friends, by relatives. America's running a Nazi racket here. All three politicians are using my stuff, from Dinkins to Cuomo to Bush.

"They're helpless men. To suck from a bright girl."

2

"The *crème de la crème.*" So President Katharine McBride had called us, that tall, commanding woman rumored to have a wooden leg, as she stood addressing us from a little hillock, at the 1960 tea for entering students. We had come together on the lawn by her house, and I recall how her gaze cleared our heads as we clustered in the hollow below her hillock. Her task, she had said, was to exhort us to the challenge imposed by our privileged status. Her words had both stirred and frightened me. Clad in my green plaid skirt and forest-green Shetland sweater, both bought specially for college, I had made my way into the library, hugging my pile of books to my chest, and had not emerged, so to speak, until the end of the first semester, when I came out with a 92 average. I had a knack for languages. For being the best first-year German student, I was given an elegant volume of the poems of Heine. We had memorized one poem in class, just a little ditty, but in the years that followed, especially when I felt blue, I sometimes intoned it softly to myself. It had a strange power of comfort.

> *Wien, Wien,*
> *Nur du allein,*
> *Sollst stets die Stadt*
> *Meiner Traume sein.*

Sophomore year, pausing to wonder why I was studying so hard, I found I couldn't answer the question. It was heady then to relax a bit, go out on dates, try out for college theater. That's when I got the part of Ophelia and studied how to seem mad. I had a crush on the senior who played Gertrude, a girl who was the epitome to me of flair and sophistication. She hardly noticed me except, so I heard, to complain to her friends that I had landed the better part. When, in despair of her liking me, one day I hit my hand against the pale green wall of my dorm room, not stopping until the poor hand was swollen and bruised, the college found out and sent me to a psychiatrist. I learned you couldn't do things like that.

We learned, too, to quote our founder, "Only our failures

marry," enjoying the breathing spell and interlude granted by this bit of bravado. All too soon—far sooner than we could imagine—the *Alumnae Bulletin* would print our new names appended to our old ones, and, by this sleight of hand, even we, the *crème de la crème*, would loom more sonorous, more substantial. "Helen Pace Minetti and Jim are both doing residencies . . . Nina Garnoff Black writes from Kenya where she and husband Dave . . ." It turned out what the founder had really said was, "Our failures only marry," though I, for one, heard this correction only many years later, at a point when at least half of those of us who had been brave or conventional enough to marry were already divorced. Unchallenged in either version was the palpability of failure. The specter of failure had always lurked as the underside of our striving for excellence.

Striving for excellence. Twenty-five years later that was still the prevailing rhetoric. Our class editor would look us over at the reunion and then write in the class notes how she saw "courage, risk-taking, determination, a commitment to excellence—all of which were fostered at this small, demanding, unrelentingly fine college."

Two of my best friends were absent from the reunion; they were among the eight members of our class who had died. As we paused to remember this ghostly phalanx, my mind retrieved what I knew of dates and causes. Mostly I knew about those who had died young. Word of these—the suicides, the accidents—gets around even if they're not friends. So I had heard about Zoe Peshka, killed the summer after graduation in a car accident in Afghanistan; and Diana Minton, careless, diabetic, not found for five days after slipping into an insulin coma—dead at twenty-three; and Roberta Kaufmann, that homely pale-skinned girl who had shared my bottle of gin in our hotel room on the junior year Geology 101 field trip to the western Pennsylvania mountains—an early suicide, though I couldn't now remember how. Tragedies, we had said at the time. Not failures. Why, I wondered, is early death a tragedy and not a failure? With all its unfulfillment of promise it might be thought a failure. And yet it isn't.

My two friends had both died at twenty-six, just four years out of college. I don't remember Alice Ames's new name, though I went to the wedding. Having trained to teach high school English and married an eager, handsome graduate of Yale Law School, she was killed with her new husband on their honeymoon in Nova Scotia. Their car collided with an oncoming truck; they both died instantly.

And Alice's roommate, Deirdre Blake, was dead a few months later of Hodgkin's disease. Ill since the year after college, she had managed to persist in her master's program in Boston at the Fletcher School of International Law and Diplomacy and in her passion for Usamah from Iraq, causing a mild ripple of scandal by sleeping with him in the graduate men's dormitory. When she came to visit me, she brought along Arab bread for her breakfast. And then she died. That death was expected, yet nonetheless a shock. I had trouble accepting it, even though I went to the funeral.With the passing of years, I still sometimes thought of my friends, Alice and Deirdre, and made up lives for them so I could retain their company. Alice would have two children and, after teaching a spell, would become a lawyer like her father, her two brothers, her husband. But she would be a lawyer who helped the poor. She would grow more deliberate, belying the college promise of a side that could be impetuous, but one could always trust in her thoughtfulness, her candor.

Deirdre's life would be more reckless. There would be a good career—perhaps an interesting post in the State Department or in international banking—but poor choices of men. She had a powerful sensuality that would keep her in its grip. Perhaps she wouldn't marry. There would be protracted but doomed entanglements. She would stand out at the reunion, still beautiful but wearing too much makeup.

Alice and Deirdre would have been at the reunion. Of that I had no doubt. Even dying young, they had launched aspiring lives.

3

I mentioned to Grace, after it was over, that I had gone to the reunion, and she asked only one question. Had I gone because my friend Joanne was going? How strange, I thought, for her to link me with Joanne, though I guess it was through Joanne that she had known me. Yes, hadn't she come once to Joanne's dorm room when I was there drinking afternoon tea? This was my other memory of her from college, which now came into focus—Grace Ellen Blau standing skittish in the doorway, one foot still in the hall, nervous, fast-talking, looking only at Joanne and not at me. Had I said something to Joanne after Grace left, indeed bolted away? Something like, "Are you friends with her? You do have a weakness for strays!" I explained to Grace that Joanne now lived in California and I rarely spoke to her. Clearly Grace didn't allow for the way our lives move on. I wonder what meaning lay for her in the passage of time—this woman deprived of those milestones of an adult life: Husband. Children. Houses. Profession. Career. Achievement. Even regrets. She couldn't say, as did Maggie Filmore, sitting next to me in the circle of classmates talking about their lives, "I wish I had been a biologist." Maggie had loved science— Biology 101 had stirred her deepest interest. But a dean had pooh-poohed her fledgling ambitions, and Maggie had knuckled under. Summa cum laude in English, a Yale Ph.D., twenty years an English professor at a midwestern state university, she still harbored the biologist within.

Maggie came to the reunion with her son, a computer science whiz, and her new, pleasant midwesterner businessman husband. Her daughter, a Yale undergraduate biochemistry major, had not been free to join them. Grace could not say, "My daughter is pre-med at Yale." Or, "We're renovating an old house in Vermont." Or even, "I sold my old house in Vermont after my husband died and I finally enrolled in law school." What was distinctive about Grace was that her life seemed to have no history of choices, right or wrong.

Yet Grace still talked about books and ideas.

"Do you know about Leibniz's theory of synchronization?" she asked me. "Leibniz was a rationalist in the seventeenth or eighteenth century; seventeenth, I think. It's synchronization that everything is synchronized in some way by some great creator. That's how the media stole my thoughts."

That I didn't put an end to the calls seemed strange to me. I told myself she was harmless. "You'll be glad to know I'm over my torture and humiliation phase," went one message. "I know you're fond of me."

And I thought, yes, in some way I am.

I was pleased that she knew this, because once, not too long before, she had castigated me for unresponsiveness. I had cut her off because I had a friend over for dinner.

"This is Grace Ellen Blau, I'm in pain . . . ," she had begun.

"I'm sorry, Grace, I can't talk now," I had interrupted to get off the phone. In a fury she had called me back.

"You don't cut off a person who's in pain. You don't do that. You know, you're a very charming person. Very charming. Very elegant. You have good manners and a lovely smile. But you can't love. You can't love."

Her words had seared. The intensity of her pain seemed

real and compelling, and her words seemed true, however
much I wondered why connection with this lunatic classmate, not even my friend in college, a person I remembered
only as sitting on a wall with her cat's eyes, or hovering nervous in a doorway, should be the test of my ability to love.

I thought she might stop calling, but she seemed either to
forgive or to forget. So there she was, a part of our lives, tol-
erated not just by me but also by my son and daughter. "Any
messages?" I would ask them when I got home. "Only Grace
Ellen Blau," they would say. "The usual weirdness." She
became a kind of family mascot—something between a
frenzied prophet and a poor relation—our own benign
crazy who commanded our loyalty and even, bizarrely, our
respect. I couldn't help feeling it a kind of sacred burden
that she had singled me out for this distinctive attention.
When the calls grew too frequent, I told her to limit them to
once a month. This gave her difficulty. She would inevitably
call more frequently, chafing against the restriction, but
once her indignation subsided, she would, thank goodness,
cut back.

I was aware that she struggled with feelings for me of
which she was ashamed.

"I have to make various things clear. This is Grace Ellen
Blau," she began one intense ramble into the machine.

"I only talk on one level of communication except for
emergency. One level. I try as hard as I can, I try with all my
strength, with all my might, to talk on one level of commu-

nication except for emergency or love, and then I fantasize
for love, but I don't mean with anyone, or not with you. I
don't talk on any level with you except the one I'm talking
on. I consider that polite. And I would consider it polite if
you wouldn't talk on any level except the verbal hard H-A-R-
D sound. Soft voices, hard sound, soft thoughts, and not on
the other level. I get very confused when people talk on two
levels. I'm not fantasizing about you, and I'm not talking
on any level except with hard sound. I can talk with a soft
voice, but in physics it's called hard sound. I'm not talking
on any subliminal level to you or fantasy level, so I'd appre-
ciate it if you wouldn't do that to me. I would find that good
etiquette."

Poor Grace. How strange, I thought, that she knew nothing about me. I understood her shame. Gertrude and the
bruised hand. I remembered, too, how back in college we
had all wondered and whispered when gawky, slightly mus-
tached Vicki Polyxides had turned up with a bouquet of
roses at dumpy Harriet Lubin's violin recital. Harriet, I
noted, was one of those classmates who brought a husband
to the reunion. I passed them strolling across the campus
arm in arm. She spoke of a college-age son attending the
Curtis School of Music.

And what life might Grace have imagined for herself? Or
still imagine? "This is Grace Ellen Blau," began one message.
"I might consider marrying you. If you'd like to come live
here with Patty, me, and Albert, her husband. He's a good

cook, he's an especial Belgian cook. She's a good nurse, and we would find an apartment for you somewhere here on Twenty-second Street, and we could talk about philosophy all the time.

"Well, if you want to marry me, let me know. Write me a note or a letter. This is Grace Ellen Blau."

Three days later, I found a second message."Maybe it would be better if I just go on dreaming about somebody I love that I speak to half an hour a month. It would be better if I just go on dreaming about somebody I love and speak to half an hour a month rather than marrying anyone. Uh . . . I do have a nurse. I couldn't fire the nurse if I married anyone anyway and . . . well, if I did marry anyone, I would marry you, that's all. I couldn't marry Joan Baez, because she's too far away, and if I did marry anyone . . . , but I'd rather just stay with the dream, someone that I love that I speak to half an hour a month. I don't think I'd ever marry anyone really, but if I did, I'd marry you and . . . , you can't rush into these things because . . . and . . . I have to keep the nurse because she's been here at least twelve years. She's married anyway—she's a heterosexual. . . . So we have to think about it for a long time if we want to get married. But probably not. Probably stay with the dream."

4

In the write-up of the reunion in the *Alumnae Bulletin* was a picture of me, in profile, talking to Linda Kretsky

Solomon. I was wearing my nice black blazer, and I thought I looked good. It did occur to me Grace might see the photograph, and I wondered how it—how I—would strike her. "I didn't want to bother you," began the message. "I know you don't want me to call you too often. You said so very clearly. I just wanted you to know that I'm feeling better. I don't feel half as deluded. Thank you for your help when I was feeling bad. I was so lonely then. I'll be getting off the Thorazine in a year.

"Your voice. You have a very charming voice you know. When you were young, you were so gorgeous. You were almost like, almost like the epitome of beauty. It almost takes the breath away how beautiful you were, around twenty, twenty-one. You still have a beautiful voice, though. And I know you have a good soul. This is Grace Ellen Blau."

After that, after the piece in the *Bulletin*, Grace began to call less often. A few messages spun out an alternative to the marriage scheme, to have me just come over and play ball with her and her policewoman friend, in front of her apartment building, out there in the street. But this as well ran into imagined complications, and she concluded it would be too difficult. Then the calls fell off, though it took some time for me to notice, given my involvements and preoccupations. Startled one day to realize I hadn't heard from her for months, I felt the sudden impact of her absence.

Grace hasn't called, but I do think about her. Was it really my picture that put her off and shattered the dream? Maybe

she just got tired of me and my guardedness, tired of the con-
straints I imposed. I can't help worrying that something bad
might have happened to her, some illness or deeper madness.
Once I got as far as trying to find her number in the
Manhattan phone book, but it didn't seem to be listed. And
I didn't in my heart want to pursue it any further.

OVER THE HILL

*T*he weather was hot and the terrain hilly as Grünli Tour
#4218 set off after lunch from Gourdon, a village north of
Toulouse, to which we had journeyed that morning by train.
Dieter, the twenty-four-year-old Austrian van driver, had
met us with the bikes, which we then tested out, complained
about, adjusted. Water bottles got filled, worries voiced
about the heat and the forty-one kilometer stretch that lay
ahead for our first afternoon; everyone was nervous and
expectant. Once in motion, however, even down that gently
sloping first hill, I knew I was fine.

On the postcard I sent to Vivyan later that evening, a view
of "Rocamadour *d'une falaise en haut*," I noted that there
were two age groups: the people in their twenties and thirties and those in their forties, and two levels of ability: slower and faster. On the whole, the younger people were the

faster riders, and the older ones the slower. And then there was me, pushing forty-nine and holding my own among the fleeter juniors. I tried to sound self-mocking; I know I was self-satisfied.

I will probably never again see Debbie, the thirty-three-year-old Canadian schoolteacher; Pam, the twenty-six-year-old television news program assistant from Washington; and tall, thin, bearded Mike, the twenty-nine-year-old engineer from Alexandria, Virginia. Yet in memory I feel them alongside me. With something like intimacy, I know the sweat on their faces, the muscles on their legs, the set of their bodies. Leslie, on the other hand, seems distant—an indistinct figure at the far end of a long dark tunnel.

It's sad to remember what good friends we were before the bike trip. First colleagues, then confidantes, we used to meet for Sunday brunch in small, not-too-expensive restaurants with a bit of charm, usually in Chelsea or the Village. Leslie was an easy person for me to get along with because I always knew where she stood. If she was tired, irritated, happy, if she did or didn't want to talk, she told me right off. And that was that; the issues were clear. I thought of her as warmly and bluntly loyal.

Sometimes, it's true, she could be sharp. I haven't forgotten the time when, trying to be helpful, I extinguished the Sabbath candles on her dining room table at the end of a Friday night dinner. I didn't know you were supposed to let them burn out on their own.

"That's presumptuous," chided Leslie, after her initial outcry of incredulity and dismay.

The word *presumptuous* swirled in the air between us. As one might with a flashlight, I searched my soul to see if I could detect a shadowy corner of presumption. I couldn't offhand, but maybe Leslie knew better. I quickly relit the candles and hoped for God's, if not Leslie's, absolution.

I forgave Leslie for calling me presumptuous because I knew her concern was for Morris. It was he who loved the observance of the Sabbath, and Leslie was protective of his needs and pleasures. Morris was Leslie's mate, and at times he seemed almost her badge of honor or her cause. They had gravitated to one another some years back at a three-day faculty development seminar on the subject of values in the curriculum. Morris, a biologist who had written on ethics, was already afflicted with degenerative arthritis, and he seemed to Leslie so courageous and impressive. They had gone to his office and made love on the floor, a piece of information that Leslie communicated early in our friendship. I also knew that Morris couldn't do it in the missionary position, but this was a spur, intimated Leslie, to their delectations at new erotic frontiers.

Leslie's confidences—boastful, exuberant, explicit—always left me uneasy, uncertain what to say to her. Most of us have made love on the floor, and probably with various partners, but I have tended to be more secretive about such instances of abandon. For one thing, some of my partners, on the floor and elsewhere, have not been men. "That gives you twice as much chance for a date on a Saturday night," said Leslie to me more than once, doing her best to cheer and urge me on. I always laughed at the joke, and for the moment joined her in believing things that simple. But I also always felt a little after-wave of depression. With her zestful, unequivocal heterosexuality, how could Leslie know the first thing about my perplexities? For me sex was too complicated to be a subject for boasting. My boasting was usually about my prowess at biking and tennis.

Leslie said Morris was a *mensch*, and I believed her. Sitting next to him at Friday night dinners, I could feel the anchor, the comfort of his warmth. It wasn't that he said much. Illness and medications combined to slur his speech, and at least in company, he left most of the talking to Leslie, who, in any case, was always so effervescent, freely trading jokes and stories and opinions with her guests. Leslie candidly admitted that in some ways her situation with Morris suited her. It was not good, she said, that Morris was sick, but his condition did leave her lots of freedom to do things on her own—to go out to dinner with friends, to attend our monthly women's poker night, even to travel. It was she who proposed the bike trip and passed along to me the brochure *Europe Biking and Hiking,* put out by a Swiss outfit called Grünli.

At first we were only humoring a fancy. In early morning phone calls—being morning people was another of our compatibilities—we reviewed the range of tours, from unchallenging Holland and "The Fabulous Loire Chateaux" (Category 1) to impossible "Switzerland's Alpine Grandeur" (Category 4). In between were "Fascinating Provence" and "Impressions of Tuscany" (Category 3). I remembered the hills around Siena and Florence, and we fixed on Category 2—"medium, a few hills. With a little bit of biking experience, it can be managed without any problems." Of the Category 2 trips to choose from, I was attracted to "Romantic Austria" or "A Hungarian Interlude," but Leslie had a strong preference for France. Finally we narrowed down the choice to Normandy, "graced by its wealth of serenity and culture," in a toss-up with the Dordogne, with its "flowing rivers, historic palaces and castles, medieval towns and villages, Stone-age grottos and caves," not to mention the "superb and delicate cuisine." Leslie and I read the descriptions aloud to each other over the phone, imagining ourselves among the apple orchards and gentle green hills of Normandy—but what if it did nothing but rain?—and, alternatively, in the Dordogne, visiting prehistoric caves and dining on foie gras and truffles.

Leslie had written on women of prehistory and was keen to visit the caves. We both liked the names of those medieval towns: Rocamadour, Loubressac, Beynac, Souillac, Les Eyzies de Taynac, Bergerac.

"Shall we put down the deposit?" I asked.

"Yes," said Leslie, "let's do it."

For Leslie's birthday that spring I made her a card, a kind of cartoon that showed two curly-headed bikers pedaling along a road—the slightly larger one was meant to be Leslie. "Leslie en Dordogne" read the caption. "*Bon anniversaire de ta copine de vélo*," read the greeting the inside.

I looked forward to the bike trip—almost passionately eager for it to start. It was strange that I should feel this way, given my lifelong aversion to organized group activities. At nine I had gone to sleep-away camp and written desperate letters home until my mother came to rescue me a week before the camp officially ended. By then, I was beginning to adjust, but docilely I left anyway. The camp awarded me the archery prize in absentia, and I kept the brass trophy on a shelf in my bedroom beneath the few blue and red ribbons I had won in horse shows and my framed certificate for out-standing penmanship. But I never went to camp, or anything like it, again. I didn't like moving with others in lock-step; I didn't like feeling compelled.

The bike tour, though, seemed to offer a set of right relations with the world. Pedaling along the roads, gazing at the succeeding vistas, I could, I felt, be inward and solitary, yet within range of other people. Maybe someone would ride beside me, but not, I imagined, for too long. As for the inns and the dinners, Leslie reassured me that she would talk to the others—she, if I liked, would talk for both of us, and I could be as quiet as I wished. As she offered me this option, I envisioned taking it and felt mousy. After all, maybe I would talk, too. But I wouldn't have to. Leslie was willing to buffer me.

"We could have gone twenty years," Leslie later said to me, after the sorry fact, as we met to talk over what had happened. We were sitting on a bench in Sheridan Square, the Union general in his oxidized dignity casting a shadow that fell just short of our place in the wan autumnal sunlight. "We could have gone twenty years without reaching the limits of our friendship."

The coming clash may have been predictable. The projected distances on the trip were twenty-five to forty miles daily, and I launched a training program that might have suited for the Tour de France. There I was each morning, carefully timing my 3.3-mile circuits of Prospect Park, pushing on the hills, extending my distances. Twice I went out to Long Island and rode thirty miles.

Leslie, meanwhile, did her sit-ups and mounted her Exercycle half an hour daily in her apartment, pedaling to tapes of Sinead O'Connor. Once she rented a bike and took it to Central Park. But the weather was excessively hot, and she didn't like the route to the park through the traffic and fumes of Sixth Avenue. "Remember," she said to me, "the trip is only a '2.' A little bit of biking experience is all you need. That's what it says in the booklet."

Our friends at poker asked if we were looking forward to our trip. "Yes," I said. "But all I'm thinking about are the distances, the hills, the heat."

"And all I'm thinking about," said Leslie—before long we

had settled into a little comedy routine—"are the inns, the other people who will be on the tour, and all that wonderful French food."

"Food? People?" I said. "What food? What people? I haven't given them a thought."

"Perhaps you'll meet someone," Leslie said to me privately.

"I seriously doubt it," I replied, adding (maybe too assertively), "and that's certainly not why I'm going."

Later, when we were on the train from Paris to Toulouse en route to meet up with the tour, it was remembering the banter at poker that led me to say what I did to the Air France pilot in our compartment. The pilot, a blandly attractive young man who welcomed the opportunity to practice his English, had chatted with us about our trip, his career, and the speed of our train, the TGV, on different kinds of rails. Then as Leslie was napping, stretched out on the seats across the aisle from me and the pilot, he turned to me with a new conversational gambit.

"Do you like French food?" he asked, carefully pronouncing each word as he flashed a winsome Gallic smile.

"I like it well enough," I replied. "But it's my friend who really likes it."

Afterward Leslie, who had not been asleep, asked me why I had said that she liked French food more than I did. Was it because she was fatter than I?

I quickly assessed Leslie's body—the square-shouldered torso, the more slender arms and legs. I hadn't intended an invidious comparison; I was just reaching for something to say. Yet as with the Sabbath candles, I felt at once guilty and aggrieved.

We had talked about competition before coming on the trip. "I don't want you making me feel bad at the end of the day if I've been slow and you fast," Leslie had declared. "As far as I'm concerned, it's not a race."

"Of course not," I had replied. "But I don't want you making me feel bad if I've chosen to push my hardest. That's what *I* like to do."

So Leslie and I struck an agreement. I could push, she could amble, and we'd meet at the end of each day's ride.

2

The swifter contingent was defined from the start, that first hot afternoon. In tandem, or at least within sight of one another's bikes, Debbie, Pam, Mike, and I rode past rolling fields of vines and sunflowers—"*tournesols*," say the French—and the occasional stone farmhouse, as far as we knew the way, then waited together for Brigitte, the twenty-seven-year-old Swiss German guide, to ride up and give us further directions. Later, Brigitte would tell us about being a guide. "First," she said in her lilting Swiss German accent, which, as you listened, softened an impression of dourness, "you meet the people, shake their hands, get a face to go with a name. Then you see how they bike, who are the strong ones, who the slower. Then you hear their stories. It's the stories that make this job worth doing. I wouldn't still be doing it except for the stories."

I suppose we added to Brigitte's stock of stories, gave her a tale or two to tell another group of bikers as they lingered one night over their espressos, became a piece of her accumulated experience, the experience that, as much as our deepening wrinkles, brings a sense of the weight of time. "I'm getting my first wrinkles," Brigitte said to me a few days later as we rode for a while side by side. "Tell me how you settled your life," she asked. Her boyfriend wanted to marry, but she wasn't sure. She knew I had two grown children.

"Well, I settled it," I answered, "but then it unsettled."

It was our first afternoon of biking, and Brigitte had a lot to do because the bikers in the rear were having trouble. "Wait here," she kept riding up to tell our contingent. We chafed at the disruption of our rhythm and chafed even more when we were obliged to take several longer breaks to allow everyone to reassemble. Aside from Leslie, the slow bikers included Isobel and Myrtle, a pair of New York schoolteachers who, like Leslie and me, were friends back home and had signed up together for the trip. Myrtle taught high school history, and Isobel—spelled with an *o*, she told us, because her parents had felt she should have a beautiful, special name—taught junior high school physical education. Myrtle and Isobel had wanted to do "The Fabulous Loire Chateaux" (Category 1), but that tour was booked, and Grünli had proposed the Dordogne as an alternative.

"I hope there aren't too many hills," Isobel had worried the previous evening in Toulouse, over *salade aux gésiers* (gizzards), a regional specialty, and lamb with a great deal of garlic.

"Don't worry, Isobel," Myrtle had answered. "If there are, you'll get off and walk."

"I guess I won't be last," Leslie had whispered to me, eyeing Myrtle.

"Aah, my thighs," now groaned Isobel, arriving at the spot where I sat in the shade of a cypress tree. "My lungs are okay, but aah, my thighs."

Myrtle was helped by her stolidness. When the hills were too much for her, she did as she had counseled Isobel—got off the bike and walked. "Just tell me the route and the name of our hotel. I'll get there," she said. "No need to wait for me." As the bikers always in the rear, Isobel and Myrtle found they didn't like the van following them in cleanup position. It was noisy, they said, and it made them anxious. So Dieter was sent on to a point ahead.

I had my own thoughts about the van. That there even was one, carrying our suitcases from one inn to the next, offering an alternative form of transportation if we needed it, offended my sense of what a genuine challenge should be. It seemed like the boat that goes alongside the Channel swimmer or the net under the tightrope. I disdained it as a hedge, almost a form of cheating. I wanted it out of sight and mind.

Myrtle and Isobel may have been struggling, but the person having the most trouble was Leslie. "I think there's something wrong with me," she said, struggling on her bike up to the resting place. As she sat down heavily beside me, her hands were shaking. "I don't think I can do it."

"Don't make any global decisions," I counseled, hoping a few right words might soothe her. "Go as slowly as you need to. And let's just take one day at a time." I patted her on the back before getting up to remount my bike.

Mike and I were the first to arrive at the little bar past the town square with the statue, where Brigitte had told us to stop. "This must be it," I said, feeling like an intrepid scout with the covered wagons coming on behind me. We took off our helmets, peeled off our biking gloves, and sat at an outside table waiting for the others to join us. I squirted the water remaining in my bottle over my head, then ordered and quickly downed two lemonades. The others were straggling in, first Pam and Debbie, then, one by one, the rest. With thirteen kilometers behind us and twenty-eight still to go, Isobel as well as Leslie now looked shaken, and Myrtle was more stolid than ever. It was at this point that the three of them decided to ride the remainder of the day's distance in the van. More hills lay ahead. A bit more difficult, said Brigitte, than what we'd done already. There would be a couple of half-hour climbs. Myrtle, Isobel, and Leslie were complaining that the level of difficulty had been misrepresented. "The brochure says this is a '2,'" they challenged Brigitte.

And Isobel and Myrtle added that they had been told it was comparable to the Loire.

"Oh yes?" responded Brigitte in her measured way, as if with a foreigner's difficulty in quite catching the words. "I think in the European booklet it's going to be a '2–3.'" The tour was a new one and had not yet been advertised to Europeans.

"I'm going to write Grünli a letter," said Leslie darkly, as she and Myrtle and Isobel helped Dieter to load their bikes into the back of the van.

Off they went, ahead of us to Rocamadour. With the security gone represented by the van, I felt both exhilarated and a little afraid. It was four o'clock. The sun beat down hard, and the countryside was vibrant in its silence. With the slower bikers gone, Brigitte, taking the lead, picked up the pace. I had felt strong over the first thirteen kilometers, but now the hills began to tire me. I realized I had started off too fast, not pacing myself for the whole day's distance. Confidence gave way to uncertainty as hills became longer and steeper and farmlands gave way to mountain scrub. Now I was regularly the last of the five bikers, arriving at the top of each hill winded and huffing and not taking long enough to rest for fear of getting left farther behind. On the second of the half-hour climbs, I couldn't keep biking and had to get off and walk. Chills were shooting up my neck. I imagined just lying down and giving up altogether. It seemed I might die on the mountain. Struggling to overcome the panic, I got back on my bike and rode very slowly. The group was waiting for me at the top.

It was now seven o'clock, and Brigitte told us that we still had an hour to go. Somehow I did it, a last long stretch, keeping up pretty well, tired but not so afraid. Close to eight o'clock we stood on a bluff overlooking Rocamadour, which lay below us, way station to medieval pilgrims, jutting yellow-stoned out of the rock face just as in my postcard to Vivyan. We swept down an arc of road. I was careful to curb my speed—the descents scared me more than the climbs— and it took my last remnant of strength to keep an even pressure on the brakes. A small final hill leading up to the town I did side by side with Debbie, pedaling in sync with her rhythm. As we put away our bikes in the garage of the Hotel Belle Vue, she offered to carry my saddle bag and water bottle. Perhaps it was the emotionalism of weariness, but this seemed so tactfully kind, I wanted to cry.

Those who had ridden in the van were gathered for a drink in the hotel garden. "I'm fine now," said Leslie. "How was it?"

I announced that it had pushed me *à la limite de mes forces*. My demeanor was calm as I concealed my secret pride. Leslie turned to Myrtle. "Do you see that?" she said. "It pushed her to the limit. This is certainly not a '2.'"

We had dinner in the garden restaurant. *Salade aux gésiers* yet again, *confit de canard*—we would eat a lot more duck before the week was out—and a wonderful raspberry

Charlotte for dessert. Still tremulous with fatigue, I sat quietly next to Leslie, who had recovered her customary verve. Later as we lay in the dark in our narrow beds, three feet apart, we talked about the biking. Brigitte had more or less assured us the second day would not be not as demanding as the first. "I'm sure it will be easier for you," I said. "In any case you can go slow. And it's no disgrace if you log some of the distance in the van."

The next morning, though, brought no improvement for Leslie. "There's got to be something wrong with me," she said as we came together for a morning coffee break. "I get winded on the least little hill." Her face was white and her hands were trembling. All I could think to suggest was that she should perhaps ride in the van and try biking again a little later, especially since we had to quicken the pace in order to be on time for a visit to Les Gouffres de Padirac, renowned stalactite caves. So Leslie, Isobel, and Myrtle all rode the second half of the morning in the van while the rest of us pressed forward under our own power.

The caves were impressive—a dark descent to a chilly netherworld of giant stalactite columns, dripping and crystallizing over tens of thousands of years. Ferried in a punt on the underground river, we glided by La Grande Colonne, which at once dwarfed us and drew us into its grandeur. Back in the sunlight, we sat outside in a garden restaurant and ate *salade au Cabecou*, a round of warm goat cheese set in some lettuce leaves. The scene is vivid in my mind, for one remembers not only the moment of crisis. Memory clings to the undisrupted flow of time leading up to it.

The projected afternoon riding was short, a distance of only ten kilometers before we reached Loubressac—"medieval town high above the Dordogne, adorned by its castle," said the Grünli brochure—and, more beckoning still, our next inn. Everyone now was biking, and I, along with the others who had ridden the whole distance, felt heavy-limbed. Leslie, though, had perked up. "You guys are slowing down now," she joked as she pedaled past me. "*I'm* fresh."

We were descending a long hill, with me following Mike and Pam and Leslie next in line after me, maybe a hundred yards back. I had just negotiated the right turn at the bottom, when behind me I heard an ominous screeching and then crashing. I turned my head and saw Leslie and her bike sprawled on the road. As she later explained when she got back from the hospital and could tell the story, her feet had flown off the pedals. She got them back on, but then slid on the gravel making the turn.

A few seconds later, we were clustered round her. Leslie lay on her back still wearing her helmet. I saw blood all over the road.

"Oh my God, oh my God," I heard myself repeating. The blood seemed to be gushing from Leslie's head and arm.

"It's not that bad," said Leslie, though it seemed bad enough to me with her lying so terribly still in that pool of blood in the bright summer sunlight.

I walked away, sat against a tree, and buried my head in my arms. "I can't carry her," I sobbed. At the coffee stop that morning Leslie had made a joke: "Let's tie a rope to your bike and you can pull me."

"I can't do that," I had retorted, smiling to cover up what for me was the horror of the thought of pulling, pulling, trying to pull Leslie up an endless hill.

"I can't carry her," I now sobbed aloud.

"Why should you even think that way?" said Myrtle, who now stood near me. "Pull yourself together. She needs you to be calm."

"Yes, yes," I said. "That's why I came up here so she wouldn't see me." I wiped my eyes and returned to Leslie's side. Brigitte was now kneeling beside Leslie, easing off her helmet and wrapping her bleeding arm with gauze. Pam was walking in circles in the road and seemed hysterical. "We've got to do something," she said. "We've got to get organized."

Occasionally, cars were passing by, and a few had stopped. "Let's see if we can get a car to take her to the hospital," I suggested. The van seemed so bumpy and uncomfortable. Pam and I talked to a young man who had stopped in a Peugeot. He was willing, he said, to go to the hospital at St.-Céré, ten kilometers away, if someone could tell him the route—he, too, was a tourist. I went back to Leslie and knelt at her uninjured side. Brigitte across from me was still working on the bandage. "You're going to the hospital," I told my friend.

"Okay," she said slowly, "but I don't have to go alone, do I?"

"Of course not," I said. I looked up at Brigitte.

"One of us should go with her," she said. "Should it be you or me?"

"You," I said, hardly missing a beat.

"As long as it's someone," said Leslie.

And that for me is the moment, something like Lord Jim's moment on the *Patna* when he froze and proved a coward, which nothing ever can undo. Brigitte and I helped Leslie into the car; then the two of them were driven off. Dieter led the way in the van, and a sorry little band of bikers followed him the remaining five kilometers to Loubressac.

"Perhaps you want to ride in the van," Myrtle said to me, her eyes scanning my face.

"No," I answered tersely. "I'd rather bike."

3

I think I knew right away, even as I chose not to, that I should have gone with Leslie to the hospital. Normally we ask so little of our friends. Do we expect them to lend us ten thousand dollars? Or to drop everything and come right away if we're sad? And yet there are moments. Leslie described them as moments when the other person should come first.

Not that she seemed at first to know she hadn't. With three stitches in her forehead, ten in her arm, and a more serious injury to her knee, which had swollen up with a large hematoma, she came back to us like a valiant, wounded soldier, and, together again in our room, the two of us looked up the French for bruises and stitches in my little pocket French-English dictionary.

"How do you say, 'I feel pain'?" asked Leslie. At the hospital she had said, "*Je sens douleur.*"

"No, no," I laughed, though I felt a little impatient with her way of riding roughshod over the language. "It's '*j'ai mal.*'"

Leslie said Brigitte had been terrific, the right person to go with her and how astute it was of me to know that. Brigitte had handled the whole business beautifully.

That night I washed Leslie's hair for her because she wasn't allowed to bathe, wiping the soap off her back with a warm washcloth. I felt tender toward her; we seemed close.

But later, months later, as we sat on the bench in Sheridan Square, we could remember only rupture and regrets.

"I reproach myself," I said, beginning with what seemed the lesser failure, "for not staying back and riding with you on the first day. Why did I have to be out front?"

"No, no, I had Myrtle," said Leslie. "I didn't expect you to do that."

"And I should have gone with you to the hospital," I said. "How could I not have gone with you? I'm very, very sorry."

"Yes," said Leslie. "I feel just terrible about that. You weren't there for me when I needed you."

"I was afraid I didn't know the system," I proffered in explanation.

"But your good French," said Leslie.

"I was so tired and shaky myself," I said. "I wasn't sure I could help you."

"If it had been your daughter," said Leslie, "you would have pulled yourself together."

Vivyan, whom I made my confidant in the long months of alienation from Leslie—the months of polite exchange, even laughter at poker, with nothing warm left underneath—said she thought I was making at once too much and too little of what had happened. I nodded my head but remained puzzled. What would have been the golden mean, the just-right way to feel about it all?

Of course, Leslie and I both looked back to the accident through the memory of what came after, the disquieting week that followed. Leslie stayed with the tour. She seemed not even to consider quitting it and going up to Paris, thinking, or at least voicing the hope, that she might be ready to bike again in a few days. To me this seemed wildly unrealistic. Certainly I considered her leaving, though I didn't know how to broach the subject. "Might you not be better off . . . ?" The self-regarding nature of such a query would have been as transparent to Leslie as it was to me.

In the days that followed the accident, Leslie felt less well. "I'm worse," she worried. "My leg hurts. The bruise is spreading." She rode each day in the van as Dieter's passenger while the rest of us biked, joining in at the stops at caves and castles and roadside cafes and in towns with the names that back home had beguiled us. It was in Souillac, I think, that my snoring made her cry; and when, in turn, her sobs woke me up, I sat on her bed and held her hand. "Why don't you phone Morris," I suggested, "and tell him about the accident?" Leslie hadn't called Morris because she didn't want to worry him. Even now she didn't, and perhaps this made her look more to me than she might have otherwise. In Beynac, Leslie snapped at me for using her bath towel, and I answered meekly that I had thought the doctor said she shouldn't get her leg wet. In Les Eyzies de Taynac I said nothing upon learning that she had used my bath towel as a bath mat, but then erupted at some later mild but insistent reproach. "Don't keep on at me," I retorted. "I don't like it." And I stalked from the room for a midnight walk around the town.

"I lay there," said Leslie in Sheridan Square. "I lay there in my bed and felt so helpless. I couldn't run after you."

"But you were being impossible," I said.

"But we weren't equal," said Leslie with great intensity.

"What do you mean we weren't equal?" I asked. "You were you, injured, and I was me, biking. What does any of that have to do with equality?"

Replaying in my own mind our words and feelings and actions, I have defended myself on point A and counterattacked on point B. By my reckoning I was nice to Leslie as often as I was distant or inconsiderate, and she, toward me, was repeatedly sharp, irritable, suspicious, resentful. I know, though, that I let her down, and not just by failing to go with her to the hospital or by falling short in little acts of consideration—for example, Leslie said I could have offered to get her more aspirin.

I let her down in how I felt about her. Though I said nothing about the accident, I was stern about it in my thoughts. It was as if we belonged to a team that *she* had let down, and I was now a critic with no mercy. She hadn't practiced enough, was unprepared, had been a blunderer. I could see her flying down the hill with her feet flapping out from the pedals, not knowing the first thing about hills or turns or anything.

I was angry at her and grew to dislike her. Her jokes irritated. Her presence seemed to occupy all the space in our shared bedroom. I hated her when she complained how Dieter had failed to carry her bag or when she mocked the French doctor, so pompously proud, she said, of his English, who had extracted the blood from her knee before it turned to the consistency of "'am."

"*Jambon?*" she had asked him.

"*Non, marmelade,*" he had replied.

"Ah, jam," had interpreted Leslie.

"*Oui,* j-ja-a-m," had said the doctor.

And my heart hardened against her, to a consistency thicker than jam. Riding by the van on my bike, I more than once kept my head averted, my eyes fixed on the road, so as not to have to catch her glance. She was like a dark shadow cutting across the sunlight. I wanted to pedal as far away as I could from her wounds, her weakness, her self-absorption, her flesh, to push up hills and swoop down into valleys, to accomplish with verve and grace each day's course, to be hardy and free.

One morning, I remember, it was raining hard, but we decided we would ride anyway and got out the bikes. I loved the whole business: of packing up the *sacoches,* the saddle bags, putting on gloves and helmet, unlocking the bikes, setting off. That day there was the added complication of the rain. Zipping up my yellow slicker, drawing its hood over the helmet, taking the gel seat covering off my saddle so it wouldn't get wet, I felt the rain not as an adversary but as part of the rhythm, the harmony. And then down we swooped, down a wonderful long hill, on into the Dordogne valley. Soon we were riding along the tree-shaded road that bordered the river. The rain, now lighter, tingled cold on my legs, but my slicker kept my torso dry. We stopped at a little chapel, warmed ourselves with a cup of tea at the cafe across the street from it, and then pushed on, wending through fields of sunflowers. The sun was now struggling to come out, but the day remained cool and everyone was biking well. After a stretch of riding, Brigitte signaled to us to stop. She, Mike, and I climbed to a lookout, below which spread the valley, the river lacing through it, a deep green vista against the lifting clouds.

And absent from all that wide expanse was Leslie—Leslie to be connected to, Leslie to remember, Leslie from whom every day I tried to hide my exhilaration.

4

"How was the bike tour?" asked Janice, at the first poker game of the fall. Glancing quickly at Leslie and then Vivyan, I stayed silent, giving Leslie the chance to be the first to answer. Leslie laughed. "Oh great," she said. "Do you know the joke, 'And aside from *that*, Mrs. Lincoln, how did you like the play?'"

By "that," Leslie explained to me on our park bench, she had meant the accident, and me. It stung to learn she had considered dropping out of poker because seeing me, she said, was painful. She thanked me quietly for my apology. Then when there seemed nothing more to say, at least that day, I remained on the bench and watched her walk away.

"I ate humble pie," I recounted afterward to Vivyan, "but it may not have been humble enough."

"What a clash of two large egos," said my daughter.

Leslie had said she was uncertain about our future as friends—we'd have to see. She phoned, though, the next day, leaving a message on my machine that our conversation had made a difference.

And two weeks later, warily hopeful, we got together for afternoon tea with Isobel and Myrtle. It was Myrtle who had suggested the reunion, Leslie and I the going out for tea.

Isobel and Myrtle had never done tea before, and they eyed the little crustless sandwiches with suspicion as we sat wedged together at a rectangular table at Tea and Sympathy on Greenwich Avenue. Isobel was describing a faculty workshop at her school in which her assignment had been to write about a day, some day in the past year, when she felt happy with herself. "And you wanna know what I wrote about?" she said. "I wrote about the bike trip. And you wanna know why? Because it was an *accomplishment.*" Isobel had a way of isolating a word and unabashedly letting it shimmer.

I glanced at Leslie and felt afraid. But when Myrtle handed her a photograph of herself in wounded splendor—Leslie seated on the grass in her bathing suit showing off her bruised arm and forehead and leg—she looked at it and gave her hearty laugh. That picture had been taken our last day of biking, the day before the tour disbanded, as we picnicked at a little lake. Leslie had not been feeling well, Isobel had persuaded her to swim, and Leslie, who loved swimming, had then felt "so much better." I remembered Isobel's self-satisfied challenge to me, "Could you have got her to do that?" And I had hugged to myself the guilty knowledge that, caught up in my efforts to evade Leslie, I would never even have thought to try.

"You know," said Isobel as we were walking away from the restaurant, Leslie in one direction and the rest of us, as it happened, in another, "I was right behind her and I saw the accident."

"Oh," I said. "Tell me about it. Leslie said her feet flew off the pedals."

"No," said Isobel. "But the pedals were going so fast, the gears weren't engaging. Then at the bottom of the hill she actually took her hands off the brakes. I couldn't believe it. She spurted forward just as she had to make the turn. She was wildly jiggling the handle bars"—Isobel clenched her fists and gyrated her hips in illustration—"I shouted at her, 'What are you doing?' And then it was too late. You know what she didn't understand? She didn't understand *momentum*. She was completely out of control."

As I now replay the scene in my mind, I see Leslie's feet on the pedals, not flying off them, and I see those pedals spinning faster and faster. I see her crouched over the handlebars, perhaps glimpsing me ahead as I make the turn. She releases the brakes, shoots forward, jiggles, starts to wobble. Everything is confused, chaotic, then violent. There is blood all over the road.

But what if then, turning round at the noise and apprehending Leslie's plight, I had rushed to her side and stayed there, without a moment's wavering? And when Brigitte had said, "One of us should go with her. Should it be you or me?" I had answered, without missing a beat, "Me"? What would have happened then?

I can see Leslie settled in the front seat of the Peugeot with me in the backseat, right behind her. I am leaning forward, one of my hands on Leslie's shoulder in a gesture of reassurance. I chat a bit in French with the young driver, helping him to figure out the route. *"Mille fois, merci,"* I thank him a half-hour later, as he deposits Leslie and me in front of the small provincial hospital in St.-Céré. Leslie hobbles along, leaning on my arm, as we make our way to the emergency room. *"Mon amie a eu un accident de vélo,"* I explain to a tidy young female receptionist, who looks up in her quizzical French way at the two disheveled middle-aged American women in biking clothes. We take our seats in a pleasant, if simply furnished, waiting room. The walls are stucco, the floor cool stone. I am there for my friend. I admire her dignity, her fortitude in adversity. The wait to see the doctor is not long.

MIND AND BODY

On my list of embarrassing secrets, only having been arrested for shoplifting at the age of twenty-seven used to rank higher than being gay. I wonder if it was even called being gay yet. I would have been the last to know, caught as I was in my secret swirl of conflict, desire, and shame. My mother used to speak of "lezzies," which for me had an unfortunate tonal association with lizards. Years later, it was my mother who made her startling attempt at consolation. "Well, of course you feel bad. It takes much longer to get over an affair with a woman than with a man."

"Why do you say that?" I asked her.

"Because women are more alike and for that reason can be so much closer," was her reply.

The question I ought to have asked was, "How do you know that?" She's dead now, and I'm left wondering. She had so many men as lovers. Why not at least one woman? But she was so heterosexual, I tell myself, just as my daughter, Sarah, is. I am reluctant to probe much further, wishing in relation to them both to retain some buffer of intergenerational discretion. My friends say it's great that Sarah, now in her twenties, feels free to share with me the details of her sexual misadventures. Meanwhile, I feel pulled by her confidences onto the wrong side of a drawn curtain. I don't want to know about the hinted-at "close call" with the Rastafarian in the park or about the more-than-close call with the man, at first so nice, who then "frog-marched" her into his bedroom.

"What's frog-marched?" I asked.

"He grabbed me by the ear and marched me along," explained Sarah.

"Oh Sarah," I said. "Couldn't you have stopped it? I take it he didn't rape you."

"No," she replied, "he didn't. But Mom, if I get pregnant . . . , would you help me take care of the baby?"

Guardedly I said I would—how could I do otherwise? I added, though, that Sarah should also put the question to her father. "Isn't he," I ventured, "the better candidate?"

My ex-husband, Richard, long aspired to be a househusband. During the years the children were small and we lived on a farm in Maine, the years they look back to as the time of family happiness, not only did he chop all the wood for our efficient Jotul stove and cheerfully join me each

Saturday on our weekly supermarket expedition, but he did so much with and for the children. Always it was Richard who drove Sarah or Matthew down the long dirt road to the pediatrician's backwoods office that doubled as headquarters for a summer campground. Then later, in New York, it was Richard, not I, who became the leading spirit of the Choir Parents Association when Sarah sang as a chorister at St. John the Divine. Predictably, also, it was he who attended not just the concerts, as I did, but even the afternoon rehearsals of the Bank Street School Brass Band to hear Matt blare his notes as one of four ungifted middle-school trombonists.

And this was the man I was said to have left for "that woman." I hadn't conceived of it as departure. Rather, I'd had in mind an understanding like Vita Sackville-West's with Harold Nicolson, though I think I underestimated the role of Sissinghurst and Vita's separate tower there, not to mention Harold's own proclivities, all of which must have helped make feasible their tolerance. We, on the other hand, were cooped up, coupled up—mother, father, two children—in a five-and-a-half-room New York West Side apartment, where, while Richard in the living room dozed over the NBC late-evening news, I would surreptitiously pick up the phone in the bedroom to murmur goodnight to my lover, "that woman."

"Matt is going to wake up one morning and say, "My

mother is a lesbian," raged Richard, in furious male alliance, when he found out. The circumstances of discovery had been so banal—a love letter not yet mailed, the envelope peeping from my unfastened pocketbook.

Richard's anger shocked me and seemed unfair. *He* didn't want passion anymore. Yet he had wept—hard convulsed sounds—the day I said I wanted us to sleep in separate rooms. "I don't know that's what I am," I answered him, numb in the face of his misery and accusations.

I felt no more a lesbian than I had thirteen years before, in 1970, when wandering into a lesbian workshop at an early Second-Wave feminist conference, I had been moved to speak as an apologist for married love. I had gone to that conference, held at my graduate school, Columbia, with my two best friends from college. Two of us had new babies and had left our husbands taking care of them at home. What an exhilarating extrication! We wanted to hear Kate Millet give the keynote address. I didn't yet realize that reading *Sexual Politics* would make it impossible ever to feel the same about D. H. Lawrence. Norman Mailer and Henry Miller I didn't care about, but I would mourn the loss of Lawrence. *The Rainbow* and *Women in Love* had seemed so thrillingly to capture the rhythms of life and love.

In a spirit of almost idle curiosity, tinged with barely repressed fear and fascination, I had made my way into the lesbian workshop, while my friends opted respectively for "Women and Finance" and "Women's Consciousness

Raising." But there I was, among women in blue jeans who were decrying the crudeness of male sexuality. Women, they said, could express sexuality in so many subtle, gentle ways. With men, it was just ramming and rape.

This seemed so wrong to me that I rose to speak. "I'm married," I said, "and I want to tell you . . . it's an extension of sexuality when my husband and I cook together. Or when we do our grocery shopping. Or when we travel, just sitting side by side in the car, and I see his burly hands on the wheel."

Quizzical glances fell on me; no one smiled. Intensely ill at ease, I stayed only a little while longer, then did my best to move unobtrusively to and out the door. Later, at the Viennese pastry shop on Amsterdam and 112th Street, at least I could repeat what I had said to my two friends as we lingered together at day's end.

My choosing the lesbian workshop wasn't meant as a personal venture or statement. At that point, ensconced in my marriage, what I called "that stuff" seemed blessedly behind me. It had always been painful, a history of confused longings. To my ninth-grade diary I had poured out my hope to be worthy of friendship with my idol, Piper Farrell, who was a grade ahead. In college I had yearned for some ill-defined response from Jane Sperling, who acted with me in college theater—Gertrude to my Ophelia in *Hamlet*, Rosalind to my Princess of France in *Love's Labour's Lost*. Finally, I had slipped into an inchoate, partial adventure at the age of twenty-five, but even that I considered romantic rather than sexual. And certainly, I didn't believe it disqualified me for men and marriage.

That it was Lucy who had suggested I marry Richard only served to underscore this ambiguity of outlook. "What about Richard?" she had said as I was complaining to her about the men in my life. "He's witty and fun and sophisticated." Did she tell me to marry him or just to take him more seriously? I can't remember. Nor can I remember if this advice was given before or after she put an end to what was happening between us.

Lucy and I had become friends in the graduate seminar on Dickens and Trollope, and even closer friends when I got involved in her abortion. At that time she was living in style off her short-term but generous alimony from her Texas oil–millionaire second ex-husband and not quite sure what to do next. Aimlessly, she had slept with a good friend's spouse; meanwhile someone had given me a phone number, reassuringly connected with a church, in case I should ever need it. Next, we were standing on her street corner, I with five hundred dollars in my pocket, waiting in the cool damp air of an early March afternoon for a green Oldsmobile sedan. We seemed caught up in the script of a grade-B movie when the metallic dark-green car pulled up at the curb and we peered through its window at a man with slick gray hair behind the wheel. "Get in," said the man, who then drove us in silence to 136th Street, a block or two off Riverside

Drive. We were directed to a doctor's office and told to wait.

It was a relief to us that the doctor seemed to be a real gynecologist. The pregnant Hispanic women filling the waiting room went in to him one by one until only we two remained. Finally, a nurse came and pulled down the blinds to the windows facing the street. Later, I remember the sight of Lucy on the table when I was allowed to go to her, and then the driver, who had reappeared, telling us where the car was parked and explaining how the three of us should leave the office, one at a time, at five-minute intervals.

That evening, while Lucy rested in the king-sized bed with the carved headboard that had been her grandmother's, I cooked dinner for her six-year-old daughter, the child from her first marriage to a college sweetheart. I was happy to be with Lucy in her house and to be useful. Two weeks later, when she went down to Mexico to finalize her divorce from the oil millionaire, she started hemorrhaging in her south-of-the-border motel room. The sheets and all the towels, she later told me, were soaked with blood.

That was the spring of 1968. A few weeks after Lucy's abortion, Columbia went on strike. Buildings were occupied, classes suspended, and I found myself spending most of my afternoons at Lucy's apartment, where, sitting together on her sofa, we drank Johnny Walker Black, listened to her Mabel Mercer record, and talked about families, friends, boyfriends, and campus politics. We both supported the students, never mind Lucy's capitalist splendor.

At a party Lucy gave in early May, her current boyfriend and I were the last guests to linger; all three of us were quite drunk. Suddenly, I was on the couch kissing Lucy, and it felt so soft. "Yes," said Lucy, "you can see why men like us." Then she said, "Let's go to bed." I don't remember where Malcolm was when we were kissing on the couch. Was he there, kissing us too? I only remember Lucy. But he was there with us in bed, doing the man's part and talking about the fulfillment of fantasy, to be in bed at once with two women. I remember his blond mustache and the smoothness of his white shoulders. Even more vividly, I remember Lucy's softness as I kissed her mouth and touched her skin, careful, though, not to touch her breasts.

In the morning, I woke up on the right edge of the bed, realized where I was, and wanted to bolt. Lucy and Malcolm cajoled me to stay for breakfast. Then Lucy said Malcolm and I should go out on a date, that we needed to get to know one another. Compliant, Malcolm later that week took me to the apartment of some friends of his, where he played a bit of poker, and I was supposed to be entertained by just sitting around and watching. That was it for me and Malcolm. Still, when Lucy and I had lunch with our friend Susan and told her what had happened, we all agreed it was okay because a man had been involved.

I'm not sure why Lucy ended things between us, whether she was afraid of what might happen next or disappointed that more didn't. There were a couple of enchanted weeks in which we used to lie together on a sofa, hers or mine, kiss, and feel all that longing. Then I spent one more night, just one, in her bed, this time without Malcolm. We were kissing as usual when she started to touch inside my thigh. If she had continued without speaking, I don't think I would have stopped her. Since she asked, "Should I do this?" I gently said no. Somehow I couldn't be the one to choose it. Quite soon after that night, Lucy dropped me for Ralph, a homely, vital friend of mine whom she had met in my apartment. Ralph would shortly espouse Marxism, abandon his dissertation on Sir Thomas Browne, and go off to work in a factory. In perfect sync with the expiration of her alimony, Lucy took to wearing chamois shirts and oxfords. No more charging at Bergdorf's.

A couple of years later, when I was safely married and pregnant with my first child, I heard that Lucy had ditched Ralph and was living with a woman on a horse farm in Vermont. Years later still, when we were both again in New York—I with two growing children and she with a different woman lover—we had lunch together at the Bank Street Cafeteria but found little to say to one another. By then, it was I who was eager to talk about the past, in search of clues to help me through the maze of present confusions. Lucy, however, had no taste for looking back.

I never told Richard about what had happened—we just didn't talk about such things—though most of my close friends knew. In 1973, I brought it up in my women's therapy group. Someone was talking about homosexuals, and I confessed to having had an experience with a woman before my marriage. To my surprise the others praised my courage and openness. I didn't tell the group about having shoplifted the nine-dollar belt at Macy's basement sale about a year before I got married. To my relief, a lawyer friend had managed to get the case dismissed.

I liked being married; it settled and anchored me. I was happy every time Richard walked in the door. So who knows how we might have gone along if Richard had remained faithful? It was after his affair with the administrative assistant in his office four years into our marriage—"betrayal" I called it when I faced him, distraught but precise, to say I knew—that I resumed falling in love with my women friends. That was also after I had read *Portrait of a Marriage* and been thrilled at the possibility of having both—the love of a man *and* the love of a woman. When I thought about being with a man, it always seemed partial and incomplete. When I thought of exclusively being with a woman, it seemed suffocating, overwhelming. I began to think that maybe I could come out right by putting the two together.

Well, I waited another ten years before acting, all the time harboring my feelings for one woman friend or another, someone invariably married or divorced and always heterosexual, telling myself I could make do with these circumscribed, romantic friendships. My desire to be with a woman sexually grew within me. Increasingly, I woke from portentous dreams, full of strangely refracted fear and longing. Meanwhile, Richard and I made love once or twice a month and learned to sidestep the fights that might have troubled our low-keyed, understated companionship.

2

And then I could tell that Julia Michaelson liked me. Her communication of this was subtle, though later she told me how she used to sit in my office—I was then an associate dean as well as a junior professor—gazing at the top of my breasts in the V opening of my silk shirt. I must admit I was a bit afraid of her. She seemed so smart, so ironic, so superior, smoking her cigarettes in a holder, never tolerating fools. I remember my trepidation when I asked the dean if she could serve on a committee I chaired. Colleagues had said Julia was a lesbian, and I was excited that she might become my lover, even if her age—fifty-nine to my forty, with her hair dyed red—gave me pause. But then she wrote me a letter saying what a help I had been to the Classics Department, asking what she could do to thank me. Could she knit me a cap? Or invite me to her house on Long Island? There was a main house and a guest cottage. I could have the main house and give elegant little dinner parties and wouldn't even know she was there in the cottage. She wants me, I exulted to myself. She wants me.

There was to be a dinner party at the dean's house, and we had both been invited.

"Will you be going?" I asked her on the phone?

"Tell you what," she said. "I'll go if you go."

"Yes," I said, "let's both go." I sat next to her at the party, aware that her leg seemed to press against mine under the table. At the end of the evening we shared a taxi. As she dropped me off, I leaned over to kiss her on the cheek. Upstairs in my apartment, I realized I was in a state of intense desire.

We arranged to go out for a drink one day after I got off from work. "This is our first date," Julia remarked in the bar of Butler Hall, not gazing out the window at the panorama of the city (as, later, she would gaze out windows with a vengeance), but with her subtly mocking blue eyes looking wryly at me. Maybe it was this evening, after all, that I was brimming with desire in the taxi home. Whichever, it seemed strange that so little actual contact—our sitting side by side, the fleeting good-bye kiss on the cheek—could have such erotic power.

A month later I was in thrall, slipping out of my house to take the Broadway bus the twenty blocks to Julia's. I felt vibrant with conspiratorial anticipation, knowing how we would kiss hello at the beginning of Julia's book-lined long hallway, then sit in the living room to have a drink or two, perhaps accompanied by peanuts—I loved the texture of these details—and then either make love, have dinner, and again make love, or simply have dinner and make love afterward. "Time for a little siesta?" she had said the first time.

We had walked around the corner from her living room into her little bedroom, each room with a splendid river view. And I had put myself into her hands.

Her hands. Waking up in my own bed after leaving hers the night before, I would remember their touch. Richard, always an early riser, would be up and about, so the bed remained my own preserve for fantasy. Eyes unopened, I would slowly inhale and try to catch back into my mouth the aftertaste of Julia's body. Burrowing into my pillow, I would pretend that I could still feel her cheek and her brow, and the hollow where her neck curved into her shoulder. I marveled that our affair had such a sureness of touch. When we first went to bed, I was always overwhelmed by the desire simply to touch her, to feel the peace that came with the delicacy of breasts touching and legs entwined, and the security of her reassuring arms and shoulders reaching round me. No man's body had ever been to me so poignantly familiar—perhaps because the focus was always so much more on the distraction of erection. And stilled by her, finding my resting place, I would think, "This is all I want. This is utter peace." Even the effort of lust seemed unwarranted. Desire would well up. I would feel its pressure in us both. But even at the most sexually extended moments, I would feel the sureness of our shared gender, knowing Julia's responses as intimately as my own, almost as if they were my own.

Or so it seemed. Later Julia would tell me that sex for her was best at its most impersonal. *Her* fantasies were of waterfalls and abstract paintings. She asked me to talk to her during sex to keep her more focused.

For those first few months, when I was swept away and felt Julia swept along with me, my obsession was how I might arrange to be with her. At home I sometimes told the truth about where I was going and sometimes lied. It was convenient that Julia was a woman—one could visit a woman friend for an evening without suspicion, particularly with a husband who got sleepy early and liked to be left alone to doze in front of the television. Worried, nonetheless, that I might be invoking Julia's name too often, I used to alternate it with that of other friends. I didn't like the duplicity (not that my scruples stopped me) and wasn't used to it either. Julia later told me that she had believed me to be a woman used to managing such complexities but that she had been wrong. She also remembered how she had warned me. "You're a married woman, darling, with two children," she had said, right at the beginning. "Can you handle this?"

"Oh yes," I had answered, without any hesitation. My working mother had taught me to say yes to challenges. "Step into the tennis ball, don't back away from it." I was all breeziness and sophistication, hiding, even from myself, that I was less experienced, more naive, and more serious than I seemed.

I had had the odd extramarital encounter with men, but these in a sense didn't count. They were little times-out from married life—passing trysts at academic conferences or on quick research trips abroad alone. Counting only a little more was my dalliance with a married lover. I had met and resisted him when I was single, able too well to envision the dreariness of watching him rise from his bed to catch the last train home to his wife and children in New Jersey. Later, married myself and living in Maine, I started seeing him on my infrequent trips to New York. I think I was both getting back at Richard—I never forgot that it was he who had broken our trust—and enjoying myself in the role of a sexual adventurer. Once I moved back to New York, though, the liaison fizzled. Neither of us wanted it to be more central in our lives.

So Julia was unprecedented—my first serious adulterous affair. I didn't think of it as adultery. It was too personal for that construction—the release of the pent-up longing of a lifetime. I wandered around in a sensual haze and felt liberated from all my shame about homosexuality. This wasn't homosexuality. Or if it was, who cared? That Julia was a woman seemed at once central and incidental. Richard cursed her as an aging hag, and I felt he understood nothing.

I tried to persuade myself that I was basically a truthful person by proving to be a bad liar. Richard was not by nature jealous or suspicious; yet even he could not overlook so much blatant evidence. He was still gracious and easy when I went off for a weekend to Julia's house on Long Island, driving me to Penn Station, urging me to profit from this nice little rest from the children. "Thanks," I said, as I lifted my suitcase from the back seat of our car; then on the train I could only think that I would be spending two whole nights in Julia's bed. Already, though, I also felt the strain. When I got to Julia's house and she was showing me round her garden, pointing out all the varieties of yews and junipers and perennials, I experienced a sharp wave of homesickness for my family. The pang passed as I entered Julia's world of mind and body.

Richard, when he knew, would lambaste Julia as irresponsible. Of course, he said, she offered excitement. *She* wasn't caring for two children. He saw her as a feckless immoralist—what audacity to call herself a student of ancient philosophy—and me as her impressionable prey.

It felt bizarre to be cast as the innocent. But perhaps that's what I was—what else do you call a forty-year-old wife and mother harboring a fantasy that she has found perfect bliss? I didn't want to make Julia my whole life, but neither could I imagine giving her up. Sitting next to her on her bed before leaving to go back home, discreetly holding her hand in the dark of the movies, dialing her phone number and feeling my heart beat as I anticipated her picking up the receiver, most likely on the third ring, I lived to be in contact with Julia and moved through life like a sleepwalker when I was not.

We were on our family vacation in Maine when Richard found the love letter in my purse. The irony didn't escape me. I reminded Richard that ten years earlier *I* had been the one to snoop and find the letter stashed in his wallet, inviting him to go off to a magic land. He had gone for a while—November to February—while I tended the two babies. I can't attest to the magic for him; for me those were three searing months, a daily struggle not to be consumed by hurt and anger. Then he came back, and I was glad of it. But I never felt quite the same about him or marriage again.

Richard said the comparison was ridiculous. What he had done was in no way like this. He ranted. I withdrew. And so began our time of great family unhappiness.

3

What followed was the end of the marriage, the end of the love affair, and, when the shock of it all subsided, the residual sense of some insight gained, though the gain seemed at a terrible cost. An analogy I at the time found fortifying, though now it seems grandiose, was to the end of a Shakespeare tragedy, that moment which is both denouement and threshold, when passion is spent, the bodies lie strewn about the stage, and the always unspectacular survivors pull themselves together to carry on.

Julia, that fall Richard first knew, happened to be away on a fellowship in Cambridge to do her research on the mind-body problem in Plato's dialogues. Refusing to give her up, I made a tenacious once-a-month weekend pilgrimage to Boston, where Julia and I would make love in her cozy Story Street sublet and go out to museums, restaurants, and movies. I clung to her and to our affair. When the moment came for me to go home, it always seemed like falling off the face of the earth. I'm not sure which I dreaded more—leaving the magic circle of warm excitement and comfort that Julia seemed to generate, or once again having to face Richard. He was drinking heavily and watching more television than ever. Turning the key in the lock to our apartment, I knew there he would be, at the end of the long hallway that led from the front door, sitting in his living room armchair, not even looking up from the TV set when I stuck in my head to say a guilty hello. What I always underestimated was how glad I would be to see the children. "Hi, Mom," they would say, as if I'd simply been out to buy milk at the corner store.

They knew what was going on. I had begged him not to, but Richard had told them. He told them right after my first trip to Boston—and in a way, who can blame him? I didn't want them burdened, but he said it was my action that was causing the burden. He told Sarah in the morning, before school, and then Matthew after school that same afternoon. The children were thirteen and eleven. What he said, I gather, to each child, was that "Mommy doesn't love Daddy any more. She loves Julia Michaelson." Sarah came to me after Richard had spoken to her. "Both you and Daddy are too proud," she said. "Neither of you can say you're sorry."

It's strange, I thought; of all the negative things I would say about myself or about Richard, being proud would not be one of them. We think we understand so much, and then find we know so little about how we are perceived, especially by our children. Later Sarah would ask me, "Who is going to take care of Daddy when Matt and I grow up and go to college?" That question shocked me, too.

Matt sought me out after school, and he was crying. "It's not true that I don't love Daddy," I said. "One can love a lot of different people. I hope you know that I love you and Sarah very much."

Sarah hated Julia Michaelson. She hated her so intensely that the next year when Julia developed breast cancer, Sarah believed her hatred was the cause. I didn't know this at the time. After Richard told the children about Julia, Sarah grew pointedly distant toward me and aloof toward everyone else. Looking at photographs of her from that time, I wonder how I failed to recognize her plight. Perhaps because it was as hidden as it was blatant. Sarah did well in school, took ballet lessons twice a week, fancied herself at once a ballerina, a potter, a karate black belt, and a writer, and honed her anger and her pain. "I hated you too," she told me years later. "I believed you had destroyed the family."

I felt as committed as ever to the family—whatever web of love, loyalties, and accommodations that term for me then signified—and clung to the hope that the children on some level knew this. At least Matt, after his initial tears, seemed undaunted, but then clearly I wasn't the best judge. He was playing forward on the junior high school lacrosse team, and either Richard or I—rarely both of us, as might have been the case in the old days of pleasure in family togetherness—would drive him to the practice or the games. "How's Julia Michaelson's cancer?" he asked once with seeming nonchalance as he dashed off with helmet in hand. It got visibly hard for him only when, finally, Richard moved out. "You were lucky," Matt said to me as I helped him pack his bag for a weekend with his father. "At least you knew who to hate." He was referring to my childhood in which I had a detested stepfather.

Then Sarah broke down. She stopped eating and marked her forehead with a razor blade. The following week, when she took a razor lightly to her wrist, she landed in the hospital. Richard carried on that it was all my fault, our shell-shocked family went into therapy, and my mother made the only reference she was ever to make to the affair, except for her astonishing consolatory comment when it was over. She told me she thought I should stop seeing Julia for the sake of the children.

Guilty and worn out, I lived for months with a taste in my mouth that I identified as the taste of panic—it lodged at the back of my throat and spread from there. I felt as if I had taken a sledgehammer and smashed up life and loved ones. But all the more I fixed on Julia. Nothing and no one, I vowed, could pressure me into giving her up.

As for Julia, this had become something other than the lighthearted caper that she, to use one of her favorite expressions, had "signed up for." I'm not saying that Julia was fickle. On the contrary, she was a loyal friend in times of trouble. But Julia was also a woman with an admirably precise sense of her own limitations. She had never lived with anyone, man or woman. She had never had a pet, unless you consider the six-foot cactus in her home on Long Island, which she had tended from its humble three-inch beginnings. And even that she eventually got rid of. "People stay with me for a while," she said, "often when they are in trouble. Then when they get stronger, they move on."

Julia's trouble—her breast cancer—came a year and a half into our involvement. During the preceding few months, though still committed to the rhetoric of lovers, we were increasingly tense and testy. Julia was making herself less available to me. Nor when we did get together was there the same spontaneous rushing off to bed. In her living room Julia had a swivel chair, in which she liked to sit and talk, cigarette holder in hand, gazing out the window with the river view. Why am I here? I would find myself wondering. Both of us looked forward to a little trip we were about to take, hoping it might restore us. The dean was sending me to London and Paris to review our study-abroad programs, and Julia had agreed to join me for the Paris segment. We had found a furnished apartment in the Marais to sublet for a week. I was elated to think I could be with Julia and do my work at the same time. We would have to be discreet, but that seemed something we could manage.

And then Julia phoned me. "There's a little problem, darling," she said. "They've found a lump in my breast. I have to have surgery the day after tomorrow."

"Oh my God," I murmured in a surge of terror and love.

I was able to bring Julia home from the hospital before I had to leave on the trip abroad. She was so happy to get back to her own place, and I remember, as she eased herself into the swivel chair, how she joked about the mastectomy, saying she might have the other breast lopped off in the interests of bilateral symmetry. There followed one bad moment, that evening at bedtime. Julia had gone into the bathroom, and she emerged from it deathly pale. "I just almost threw up," she said. The bandages had been removed before she left the hospital, and in her own bathroom mirror she had looked for the first time at the long red sickle of a scar.

Also, for the first time since I had known her, Julia was wearing a nightgown, the one she had bought for the stay in the hospital. That broke my heart. The Julia I knew slept naked and had taught me to sleep naked as well. "Julia," I said, "you don't need the nightgown."

"Oh, all right darling, whatever you say."

I took her to bed, carefully removed the nightgown, and then gently, very gently made love to her. At one point Julia cupped her hands over her eyes and held them there a long time. "Thank you darling," she said at the end. "It's nice to be feeling something pleasant."

The moment in the bathroom was Julia's one visible lapse

from fortitude in the whole ordeal of having cancer. Whether by upbringing or nature, Julia was stoical. I had a theory about her extraordinary coping that helped me to understand it without lessening my admiration. I think we all have a point in our past that remains the age of our self-image. For Julia, it was ten, the year her father died and she cut her hair short and became a committed tomboy. Maybe for Julia, breasts weren't really part of her core sense of self. Or so went my theory. I don't know what it has felt like for her to wake up every day without one.

I missed Julia's breast but was careful not to show it. I had loved to burrow my face between her large soft breasts, wrapping them around me like earmuffs. Now I lavished on the survivor the attention that had been given to the pair. It seemed, though, strange and lonely.

The six months of chemotherapy were dreary, but Julia soldiered on. She lost most, though not all, of her hair and continued to dye red the little that remained. She tried smoking marijuana to combat the nausea. She taught her classes, chaired her department, and complained about her lack of energy. Work on the mind-body problem did not advance.

We soldiered on too—I pressing and Julia withdrawing—and then ended the affair at more or less the same time as the chemo ended. Julia had a grant to go to England. We talked vaguely about my visiting her, but both knew I wouldn't. By that time, Richard and I, too, had separated. He had moved out, renting a small nearby apartment, while I maintained our old home for the children. Sarah had recovered from her crisis and gone off to boarding school. Matt, living at home, had become a truculent teenager, doing his schoolwork in a grudging though minimally adequate way and needing a parent's vigilance. He was angry with me for having "messed up." Without apologizing, I did my best not to compound the mess further.

Julia was away, and without hope or even desire for our future, I missed her. On the alternate weekends that Matt spent with Richard, I used to go to her country house to tend her shrubs and flowers. Sometimes I browsed through the box of her childhood photos, which she had shown me in our early love-struck days. There was little Julia, aged nine, with her blond ringlets, sitting with her beloved father, who would die within the year. He had been gassed in World War I and never fully recovered. There was Julia, aged ten, her hair cut short, standing with her two brothers. Then there was Julia as a buoyant, sexy young woman. And her boyfriends and lovers: the German Jewish immigrant violinist, touted to me as her first love; the professional mentor, so much older than Julia, who had wanted to marry her but then died; the key woman lover, a brilliant but tragic alcoholic, whom Julia had always looked out for, though the passion, she said, had waned long ago. "Tell me about the past," I had so often urged her. And she had spun the tales of old love affairs. Is it, I wonder, just an extension of possessiveness to wish to have known the person younger? Photos of Richard young had inspired in me the same wistful pressure of feeling. With Julia, though, I think I shifted from wanting to be with her to wanting to be her. Or at least to be more like her. I admired her life. Julia and her sixty-year-old friends were impressive—they had done their jobs, bought their country houses, and were independent women. Julia seemed the least trammeled of the lot—no parents, no children, no pets, no abiding partners. I came to feel a little sorry for her, but at the same time she inspired me.

4

July 1996. I am sitting with seven other women at a dinner party in Noyac, Long Island. One of these is my lover, though I do not call her my partner. The remaining six are three lesbian couples. We are all about the same age—late forties, early fifties—and all, except my lover, who is my guest, own country houses in the area.

Only one other woman has children as I do, and she and I trade stories. The woman tells how her son at first hated her lover. He was fifteen then and had been rude as only a fifteen-year-old boy can be. That night she said to him, "I'll always love you best, but don't you want to have your own life?" After that, she says, he was fine. He and the lover are now great friends. I, in turn, tell her about my daughter, how a couple years back I said to Sarah, when she was complaining about one of her boyfriends—the one who had wanted to do S & M but, thank God, she wasn't interested—"You're thoroughly heterosexual, aren't you?" I tell the woman what Sarah said in response; it gladdened me so at the time and still does. Sarah said, "At least until some woman tempts me." That seemed such a wonderful untroubled statement after all we had been through. I tell her, too, about Matt, when he was in college, calling me up in great excitement to tell me that Julia Michaelson's article on the mind-body problem was on the syllabus in his Principles of Knowledge course. "She's a really well-known scholar, Mom," he eagerly informed me, as if I didn't know. Not to be misleading, I add that it also was Matt who said to Sarah after Julia had come over once to have a drink in our apartment. "I know it's not right, but I'll always think of her as the villain."

The women at the table start talking about when they knew about themselves. "I always knew," say several. "I just didn't act on it until . . ." Eighteen or twenty-seven or thirty— as one would expect, the age varies. "I always knew," agrees another. When they were both students at Vassar, she went with her lover to spend the night at the Plaza Hotel in New York. "Did you really?" I exclaim. "How wonderful! What boldness!"

"And what about you?" this same woman, now a successful money fund manager, asks me.

"I'm not sure I know now," I say. "But I took the plunge at forty after fourteen years of marriage."

The word *bisexual* is on my lips. It seems as good a term

as any, but I hesitate. Not that this label doesn't fit best, given my history and abiding sense of possibilities. I still imagine making love to men, and I do believe I could love a man again, even though I'm totally out of practice. It's just that labels seem so limiting and encoding, so remote from what actually happens. They leave too much out, though I suppose I'm willing to call myself an English teacher, a mother, or a woman, with far less need to equivocate.

I smile at my dinner-table neighbor, conveying my semi-apology for a difference in certainty I hope won't estrange us. She smiles back, and I sense her effort to be tolerant. If I knew her a little better, I might tell her my love stories.

THE BAD HAND

Vivyan was still a member of the poker group when we changed from "winner-take-all."

She had been discreetly scornful of our peculiar way of playing. "It's not real poker," she took some relish in informing me in private. "But promise me you won't say anything. I don't want to upset the group."

Vivyan had played a lot of poker, real poker, when she lived with Michael. Michael had been her lover for fifteen years—her twin, she said. They both loved words and literature. They had recited to one another the names of exotic places.

Finistère.

Ootacamund.

Troviastpul.

Michael had been a Harvard senior, and Vivyan, five years older than he, a graduate student in comp lit (she knew

English, German, French, and Russian as well as her native Swedish), when, by her account, she had set out to seduce him because of his extraordinary blue eyes. Vivyan's son, Tom, was then an infant, but Vivyan had relinquished him to the care of her own mother back in Sweden. Vivyan remained the baby; actual babies scared her, and she didn't want to have one. Going to see her son in her parents' comfortable home, the home of her own childhood, she could imagine herself his sibling. Meanwhile, "Tom's father," as Vivyan invariably referred to this devalued figure in her private mythology, had already faded into the background: he was the out-of-touch former husband who had moved halfway round the world to South Africa.

I never knew a name for Tom's father. Michael's name was another matter. "Michael," said Vivyan, and the syllables shimmered sensuously and distinctly, the first a proclamation, the second a caress, ending with the lightly pronounced *l*. Vivyan seemed to expect the listener to know Michael's importance.

I encountered Michael only once when he and Vivyan had a rendezvous at the White Horse Tavern on Hudson and Eleventh. Vivyan needed to pick up the key in order to water Michael's houseplants while he, his wife, Emma, and their new baby spent the summer in Paris. Vivyan often told the story of how Michael had been entrapped by Emma—"his student," said Vivyan, with a fillip of contempt—after Vivyan had at last walked out. "I would go to the movies," she confided, "to get away from his drinking and his terrible depressions. One day I couldn't bring myself to go home."

Vivyan and I had been out on one of our walks, and she had asked, as if offering me a special bonbon, if I wanted to meet Michael, ever her loyal friend.

"Oh yes," I said eagerly. Michael was sitting at one of the outside tables smoking a cigarette and reading the Pléiade edition of the poems of Gérard de Nerval. Vivyan always stressed how fat he had grown, how dissolute, how altered from his handsome younger self, so I was surprised by how handsome he remained. He raised his blue eyes from the book as Vivyan introduced me, and I felt myself held for a moment by their gaze. Michael's manner was pleasant though in no way effusive. I stayed only to say hello, then left him and Vivyan, sitting with the table between them, as I walked away to the Christopher Street subway.

By then I knew Vivyan's assertion—it had been one of her earliest confidences to me as we began to trade accounts of our lives—that she had never in the past had women friends. Her friends had been either Michael's friends or her Harvard male students. The way she lingered over the names—Ben, Theo, Eric, Charles—seemed to endow each figure with an aura of romantic possibility. These had been the other players in Vivyan's earlier poker games.

Even when she walked out on Michael in order to be with Louise, this didn't, Vivyan said, mean a preference for women. In any case, Louise seemed someone who eluded normal categories. *"Ce n'est pas une femme,"* pronounced Vivyan's sister at the end, the sad end of it all, in the one language in which we could carry on a conversation. She paused for a moment. *"Ce n'est pas un homme non plus. C'est un bête."*

It wasn't the poker unprofessionalism of winner-take-all that bothered Vivyan most about our game. The thing she disliked, I should say despised, was what she perceived as the group's backbiting. When Janice had twice canceled on the day of the game, leaving Miriam not enough time to find a replacement, Miriam had wondered (just a trace acidly) whether Janice herself ought not to be replaced.

Nothing had come of this. But Vivyan, who hated conformity and constraints almost as much as she hated meanness, assumed in her mind the role of Janice's champion. "I really like Janice," she would say to me whenever we started talking about poker. "If they kick Janice out, I'll leave too."

Janice stayed in the group, as did Vivyan, and we continued to meet each month with the same effusive declarations of what fun we had playing poker. We talked about movies we had seen and joked about sex we had or hadn't had, with what seemed the old panache. For example, there was the evening Bitsy told us about her friend who had slept with Bitsy's twenty-year-old son, Nathaniel. That was the same night we had discussed *Silence of the Lambs.*

"I was very upset," Bitsy said about her friend. "It seemed such a betrayal."

"Why?" asked Vivyan, looking up with interest from her cards, her mouth curving into a quizzical smile. Both Vivyan and Leslie confessed to their lust for my son, Matthew. "You should see him," said Leslie to those who hadn't had the pleasure. "The sexiest nineteen-year-old I've ever laid eyes on!" I then confessed to my warm appreciation of Vivyan's twenty-four-year-old son, Tom. Tom had come to New York to study architecture, and when I met him at Vivyan's one warm summer day, I had admired his beautiful arms. Leslie and I quickly added that we would never act on our fantasies. Vivyan, however, saw no reason why we should restrain ourselves. Why should Bitsy mind her friend's dalliance? She claimed that she, Vivyan, was not a possessive mother, and challenged me, or any one of us, to seduce Tom if we could. I barred her from seducing Matthew but felt bourgeois and ungenerous to be declaring him off-limits.

Banter drew us all in, but poker, I think for all of us, was less exciting than it had been in the beginning. Anaconda to the right or left no longer had quite the same thrill. Bitsy's soybean casseroles, while still delicious, had become predictable.

It was then that Leslie and Miriam, joined by the rest of us, began to think of changing from winner-take-all. Winning the whole pot could be exciting, particularly for the winner. Still, I, for one, always felt guilty, pocketing thirty-five dollars while everyone else went home with nothing. More of a problem, winner-take-all encouraged reckless betting on the last couple of hands. Why not bet high if you had nothing to lose, having lost already, or if your only chance of winning anything was to build up an enormous pot on the last hand? It may be odd to appeal to fairness in a game of chance, but it did seem unfair that after one person had been steadily ahead all evening, someone else could snatch the victory by winning just the final round.

"Winner-take-all does skew the betting," admitted Bitsy.

"But if we're going to play the regular way," said Leslie, "we need to work out a formula for what chips will be worth. And we've got to go to more than nickels and dimes."

"Leave it to me," said Miriam. "I'll run a plan by you next month."

At the following month's game, Miriam handed out a sheet of paper that set forth the values: white chips would equal a quarter, red fifty cents, and blue a dollar. Each player would buy ten dollars worth of chips at the beginning of the evening and then at the end take back from the bank whatever her pile amounted to. Sitting that evening at the head of the table, near the little side table on which we put the money, I volunteered to be the banker. At the end of the evening, busily counting out bills, asking people for change, I saw that the money got distributed—$16.25 to Leslie, $12.50 to Miriam, $8.00 even to Vivyan, $4.75 to Janice, and so on. I always felt too eager at such moments and admired Vivyan's detachment, her class. It didn't seem to matter to her whether she won or lost or whether she got exactly her due. She certainly wouldn't have asked, as Miriam did, for the odd fifty cents.

The group agreed that the new system worked and that we liked it.

"It's much better," Vivyan repeated to me privately. "I didn't want to say anything, but the other wasn't real poker."

Vivyan, nonetheless, was voicing strong reluctance about continuing in the game. All her life, she told me, she had resisted commitment. She needed to feel free to follow her whims, to get on a plane at a day's notice to fly to New Orleans, where her former student Charles kept begging her to visit, or at the last minute to cancel an evening's dinner date, pleading a headache, or one of her stomachaches, or just low spirits.

"And people can cancel on me," she said. "I don't mind." It was Vivyan's theory that almost everyone is always on the verge of canceling, so when one person actually does cancel, she is really doing the other person a favor, letting him or her off the hook. What Vivyan liked best, or so she said, was to walk from her apartment to Balducci's, buy her piece of fresh salmon or snapper, interrogating the fish-counter man as to its freshness, move on with the same critical eye to inspect the produce, choosing perhaps a couple of new potatoes and a head of broccoli, stride forth to the video store on Hudson to rent a film, and then go home to be her own company for the evening.

"I could easily become a hermit," she told me.

I never quite believed in Vivyan's professed passion for isolation. To me she seemed a little coy, willing to cancel on her friends and hold them at bay but still needing to find their messages on her phone machine. "I had seven messages," she would typically complain. Then she could marvel that the friends kept calling when she did so little to encourage them.

It was June when Vivyan really did drop out of poker, right before she was leaving for Paris to teach a six-week summer school course on French and American writers of the Twenties, her one annual "commitment." This year the usual frenzy of departure was intensified by the uncertainty of her New York living situation. Having given up the apartment she had shared with Louise, she had moved into Michael's place while he and his family were still away on his sabbatical. In the fall, though, they would be returning, and Vivyan needed to find a new home. Between apartment hunting and preparations for leaving town, she felt too harassed and unsettled for an evening of poker. A last-minute call to Miriam set the seal on her resolve to quit for good.

Miriam told us she had not let Vivyan off easily. Vivyan's account was that she had politely urged Miriam to find someone else. "If one needs to be that regular," she said to me, "I can't be counted on. I'm going to Paris. I may at any point go to New Orleans. It's not fair to the group if they need me to tie myself down."

Miriam rustled up a friend of Leslie's as a replacement, a perfectly pleasant woman who worked in banking and whose jokes grated on me all evening. I missed Vivyan that night, and I missed her in the fall when she didn't rejoin the game. I even thought of quitting myself, but I have what seems to me a boring tendency to stick with what I start. Maybe it seems boring only because someone like Vivyan, with her disparagements of regularity, can make me feel that my routines are tedious. It's as though she could have done everything I have done—been a tenured professor, a dutiful mother, a continuing member of the poker group—but was saved from so pedestrian a fate by her constitutional superiority to the mundane. Oddly, what you might consider failures in someone else, or at least incompletions, stood out as Vivyan's badges of honor.

2

Vivyan's second great love, the love that came after Michael, was Louise. I first heard about Vivyan and Louise from Wanda, who had met the two of them at a writers' convention in Finland. Young, French, androgynous, and very clever, Louise had published a novel in which it was impossible to determine the narrator's sex. The book had enjoyed a moment of critical acclaim in France. It was the story of the narrator's love affair with a black transvestite.

Vivyan had been forty-two and Louise twenty-three when they had set up house together on Horatio Street. The apartment was ordinary, but Vivyan liked to take you into her study and direct your gaze out the two big windows.

Looking westward and skyward, you saw the billboard with an ad for Maxwell House Coffee. Looking north and down onto Gansevort Street, you could watch the transvestite hookers. Vivyan loved the billboard and the transvestites. They defined the boundaries of her home, her haven. To me, she seemed the most romantic and the most despairing person I'd ever known.

Vivyan spoke gently of Louise's vulnerability. Louise had fine blond hair that framed her long, pale, Gallic face. She was persuaded that she was a genius and that Vivyan was one as well. I met her when she and Vivyan were still together as lovers in the apartment. "My roommate," said Vivyan by way of introduction. When Vivyan took a cigarette out of a pack of Camels, one of the three cigarettes she allowed herself each day, Louise whipped out a lighter, struck it alight, and held out the flame.

Already Louise had betrayed Vivyan—I knew the story from Wanda and then, much later, from Vivyan herself. The crisis was two years in the past—and three years into their history. Louise had been careless about the phone calls. They had turned up on the common bill. Louise had lied, but somehow Vivyan had also discovered the letters. It was the letters that hurt most. Sex was nothing, but she could not forgive promiscuity of words.

"Louise is insecure," explained Vivyan when we came to talk about such things. "She has to seduce. It's her mission to rescue every woman that she sees. I will never trust her again." It was only a few months after the betrayal that Vivyan, ready, as she said she was, to leave Louise, had been deflected by a great crisis. She had been diagnosed with colon cancer—though at an early and operable stage. Her mother had come from Sweden to take care of her. Louise, too, had been totally devoted and later, after the surgery, when Vivyan was recovering, had implored forgiveness. "On her hands and knees," said Vivyan.

So Vivyan and Louise clung together, and by Vivyan's account they were unhappy. Louise worked at her writing late into the night, slept all day, and when she was awake, read books and chain smoked. Vivyan was never still—her long hands, if not the rest of her, would be in motion—while Louise lay for hours reading on the black living-room couch, a pillow behind her head and a full ash tray on the coffee table at her side. She seemed still the way a snake is still—emotionally coiled, ready to strike. Vivyan and I, introduced to one another by Wanda, had become friends and used to take our walks. She was proud of her long quick stride and would make no concession to my shorter legs. Scurrying along beside her, I listened to her talk. "There are only two great American artists," she pronounced one April afternoon as we crossed the Brooklyn Bridge, midpoint on a seven-mile trek that took us from Vivyan's apartment on Horatio Street to mine in Park Slope.

"Who are they?" I asked, uneasy in my blankness.

"Georgia O'Keeffe and Richard Diebenkorn."

"Oh yes?" I said, at a loss what to say next.

Wanda and I talked about Vivyan. "She can't cope," said Wanda. "She's a brilliant neurotic woman who can't cope. Her opinions are just bluster."

In my apartment that day of the long walk, sitting with me on my sofa and looking at my albums of childhood photos, Vivyan softened. She laughed appreciatively at pictures of my pretty mother and of me as a baby. I asked if she would like to stay for dinner, but she said she needed to get home to dinner with Louise. When she left, I felt a little blue, yet happy, too, to think of my odd new friend.

Vivyan's talk, at this time, was of her looming separation from Louise. Louise was returning to France on a year-long leave of absence from her teaching job at Yale, and she and Vivyan had decided to let their lease expire that December. Vivyan could camp out for a time at Michael's. When Louise came back, Vivyan said, they would not live together again.

Meanwhile Vivyan and I took our walks, mused about places and language and literature, and sometimes went to the movies. Once, shortly before she left for Paris, as we were walking along Hudson Street, having just had tea together at the Cafe Sha Sha, I took hold for a moment of her hand. Later, from Paris, where Louise was still making her miserable, she wrote me that she could use "a squeeze of my little hand." I was thrilled. But that's as far as anything ever went between us.

"I wish I could be a lesbian," said Vivyan, but she insisted it was not her bent. Louise, she said, was not like any other woman. As for me, I spent hours lost in gentle fantasies of Vivyan, but looking back, I think these fantasies contented me. Somehow they were enough.

The following fall, Louise did stay on, as planned, in France, but kept coming back for little visits. She was in New York at Thanksgiving and came along to the Thanksgiving dinner at my house that Vivyan and I had planned to have together with our children. Vivyan loved Thanksgiving; she held forth at length about mince and pumpkin pies.

"But I can't leave Louise alone at Thanksgiving," she explained to me, when it was clear that Louise would be in town.

"Bring her along," I answered, trying hard to work up a spirit of holiday inclusiveness. For good measure I invited my ex-husband, Richard.

"How was Thanksgiving?" an inquisitive Wanda probed in its aftermath.

"Fine," I said. "Louise and Richard hit it off very nicely."

"You're amazing," laughed Wanda. "Going to all that trouble."

Next, Vivyan and Louise planned to be together in the summer when Vivyan would go to Europe again to do her teaching. By now I had talked myself out of any hopes, even any secret wishes, that Vivyan might be other than a friend to me. The transition had been discreet and fluid. Nothing had ever been declared, at least nothing pointedly personal.

"Friends," said Vivyan, as one of her emphatic opinions, "are far more precious than lovers."

3

Before she left for that second summer in France, around the time she dropped out of poker, Vivyan began her search for a new apartment. She had money in the bank from the sale of family property in Stockholm, enough to fund an all-cash purchase of an elegant two-bedroom New York condominium. Vivyan's idea was to sink the money into the apartment and rely on her wits as a journalist, translator, and writer to make the small income she needed to live on. She kept calling to enlist me to help her look, and usually I would say yes, ever willing, even eager, to hop a subway to the Village, Soho, Tribeca, or Chelsea—though Chelsea for Vivyan was stretching the limit—to inspect yet one more possibility.

I liked the condominium on Perry Street—it had such wonderful light and big square rooms—but Vivyan worried someone might build across the street.

"And what would the apartment be without the view?" asked Vivyan.

She said she liked the rather stark new renovation on Duane Street in Tribeca, across the street from the Duane Park Cafe.

"I think it's fine," I said, "though I guess I liked Perry Street better."

"But this is better value. Don't you agree?" said Vivyan. "Really there's no comparison."

"This is very nice," I said.

"Ugh," said Vivyan. "Every time I come close to buying, I want to get on a plane and flee."

When she thought her Duane Street bid was going to be accepted, she stayed up all night worrying, and her stomach never stopped aching.

We even talked about sharing a house or a duplex— Vivyan would take the top floor or floors because she loved light so much. I also loved light, but it was more important to me to accommodate my friend.

"You could sell your apartment," said Vivyan, "and your share would be only $290,000."

In my mind I quickly totaled my resources, though the exercise wasn't required for me to know the venture was out of the question. To Vivyan I nodded with a circumspect smile.

For Vivyan, there was then the loft on Mulberry. An engineer had inspected and approved; Vivyan's son, Tom, the architecture student, was set to build the room divisions and cabinets; the lawyer was checking out the contract.

"I'm a wreck," said Vivyan, "but this is it. The contract will be signed day after tomorrow."

As always, something went wrong. The deal snagged and crumbled. Vivyan took to not answering her phone in order to dodge the realtors. "They don't leave me alone," she said. "My message machine is glutted with their calls."

When Vivyan finally left for Paris, I felt relieved. The apartment search had seemed to be something real, and I was coming to understand that it wasn't. Or perhaps *real* and *not real* are the wrong terms. I think looking to buy the apartment was Vivyan's metaphor; her inconclusiveness was her expression of resistance and of despair. I say this, though, only in hindsight. At the time Vivyan's fruitless, agitated quest left me frustrated and perplexed. I don't mind "wallowing"—Vivyan's word—in hope and illusions, but I'm eminently practical when something really needs to be done. And didn't Vivyan have to have a place to live?

Vivyan and I exchanged a postcard or two over the summer but otherwise were not in contact. Then a phone call in late August tracked me to the house I had rented on Cape Cod.

"When you come back," said Vivyan, "I'd like you to come with me to look at some apartments. I'm desperate now, truly desperate to find something. Can you believe Michael? He has moved up his return because Emma is tired of Paris! *Quelle bourgeoise!* I have to be out of here by October 11, and when I told him I needed an extra week, he said no."

"What a dog," I said, trying to conceal my secret sympathy with Michael. Yet I was drawn back in to Vivyan's plight and flights of fancy.

It was Wanda who told me that Vivyan and Louise were truly finished. Vivyan had arrived in Paris to find Louise paying court to the wife of the director of La Societé des Arts et Lettres, to which Louise was attached as a visiting scholar.

"A mincing, desiccated *bonne mère de famille*" was the way Vivyan later described her rival.

"And Vivyan says this is it," reported Wanda. "They're finished."

"Do you really think so?" I asked. I couldn't help feeling gratified.

I dined with Vivyan in late September, and we talked about apartments. There was a loft in Soho on Mercer Street, but Vivyan wasn't certain about the neighborhood. Would I go with her to look?

"And Louise?" I finally asked.

"She's back now," said Vivyan, "and keeps calling. I refuse to see her, though I guess one day she'll have to come and pick up her books."

"Are you all right?" I asked.

"Yes," said Vivyan. "At first I suffered terribly. But I'm amazingly all right." She flashed her winning smile as she clasped and unclasped her long hands.

"Why don't you rejoin the poker game?" I asked. "I miss you there."

"No, I don't think so," said Vivyan. "I'm probably going to New Orleans next month. I don't mind filling in, but I don't want the regular commitment."

4

The next time I saw Vivyan, in early November, she was living in a dilapidated two-bedroom apartment on West

112th Street and Riverside. Plaster was falling from the ceiling, but light poured in the windows of the large, high-ceilinged rooms. The apartment belonged to a friend of a friend, someone who had moved downtown but was retaining this place for visiting relatives while waiting for the real-estate market to improve.

Vivyan had had to scramble to move from Michael's. She had found a one-week sublet in the same building and then, serendipitously, the Upper West Side rental, which she had been able to take month to month.

"You always land on your feet," I said, admiringly.

"Yes," said Vivyan, as she poured my favorite herbal tea, Almond Sunset, from her own little white tea pot into one of the utilitarian gray mugs belonging to the dilapidated apartment. "But this time it was a close call. Three days before having to leave Michael's, I had absolutely nowhere to go." She dunked a peppermint tea bag for herself into a second mug.

Vivyan was still looking to buy an apartment, but her more urgent agenda was escape. It was only the severity of her stomachache that was keeping her from taking off for a month in New Orleans.

"I'm going to have some tests," she said. "They think I may have an ulcer. If everything is okay, I'll be off a week from Wednesday."

As for Louise, it seemed she had been very sweet in helping Vivyan move. They had spent a couple of weekends together, though strictly, said Vivyan, as friends. Louise had rented an apartment of her own in New Haven.

After our tea Vivyan and I went out for a walk. She had found the local food shops and video store but didn't know about Oppenheimer Meats on Ninety-ninth and Broadway. We walked down Broadway to the famed local butcher, and Vivyan bought a Cornish hen for her dinner. She invited me to eat with her, but I had another date. I left her on the corner of Broadway and 112th with her little bird in one bag and the two videos she had rented for the evening in another.

"Be good," said Vivyan, as always. And we kissed on both cheeks as always, right-left-right.

I was surprised over Thanksgiving and into early December when Vivyan didn't respond to my phone messages. I thought it likely she was seeing more of Louise. Finally, I reached her.

"I was planning to call you," she said. "But you'll understand why I didn't."

The tests had showed a recurrence of cancer. This time in the liver.

"Oh my God," I said. My hands were cold. I didn't know what to ask next.

"Yes," she said. "At first I was devastated. *Tu peux imaginer!* But it's good that it's not really liver cancer. It's colon cancer that has traveled to the liver."

"Aha, that's good," I repeated, trying to share Vivyan's

perspective. "And treatment. What's the treatment?" I clung to the American notion of recovery.

The treatment was a chemotherapy injection that could be given in the doctor's office once a week. Vivyan was to start the following Monday.

"Have you told Tom?" I asked.

"Not yet," said Vivyan. "He's coming to dinner tomorrow." Vivyan's parents had flown in from Sweden and were staying with her on 112th Street.

I went to see her two days later, and we all sat in the living room holding our mugs of tea—Vivyan, her mother and father, and I. It was hard to know what to say. Vivyan seemed at once to want and not to want to talk about her illness.

"How are Sarah and Matthew?" asked Vivyan's mother, a tall, dour woman clad in a sensible tweed skirt, who always inquired about one's children, as if the very question had power to right our lives' shadowy turns. She had been striking when she was younger. Vivyan had shown me pictures. I talked a little about Sarah and Matt while Vivyan, next to her mother on the sofa, crossed her arms over her chest and cradled her elbows in her long hands. We spoke as well about Vivyan's stories—how good they were. Vivyan's father, a noted journalist, said he wanted to translate them into Swedish. When Vivyan went into the bathroom, he looked at me, stricken. "How terrible this is," he said.

I had a sense of the apartment as a waiting room. In it sat Vivyan, her mother, her father, all waiting—waiting for the treatment to start, waiting for knowledge, waiting for Vivyan's cure and for her death. All daily occupations of eating talking, sleeping, had been leveled out to the act of waiting. Finally, Vivyan proposed a little walk, since she and her mother needed to shop for dinner. "My mother's going to buy me a new coat," she said as she put on her familiar frayed one.

We walked three abreast down Broadway to Oppenheimer's, where Vivyan and her mother talked over what to get and decided on some lamb chops. Vivyan then sent her mother home with the package of meat, saying she would walk a little more with me.

"Where would you like to go?" I asked.

We went one block east to Amsterdam, then headed back uptown. "I'm not tired," said Vivyan, "but I'm terribly cold. It's horrible when your body turns against you."

I asked about Tom.

"We told him," said Vivyan. "But he didn't really seem to understand that it's serious."

The word *serious* jolted me.

When we got back to Broadway and 112th Street, Vivyan asked me if I would like to come up again to the apartment, but since I didn't want to intrude and I was worn out from the undertow of sadness, I declined.

"I'll come again soon," I said. We made a plan to play Scrabble. Vivyan liked to boast that she could regularly beat Louise in French Scrabble. I said she was sure to beat me in English.

5

The first oncologist refused to treat Vivyan because her insurance did not cover his fees.

"You wouldn't believe such an idiot," Vivyan said to me over the phone. "I told him that I had the money. But he wouldn't take me."

"That's outrageous," I replied, suddenly afraid chemotherapy might prove as elusive as the hunt for an apartment.

Vivyan, though, did start the treatments. I would call her, waiting a day or so after each injection so as not to disturb her too soon. Gone was the spontaneity of picking up the phone to chat about this or that. Now there was only the one subject; we broached it with needful matter-of-factness. After the first injection Vivyan was pleased to say she felt only a bit peculiar. After the second she was relieved and even sanguine—her stomachache had gone away. A few days later, however, she reported a strange rash.

I wanted to see her, but she expressed reluctance. "I'm all red and puffed up," she said. "Let's wait until the reaction subsides." Also, she was very busy, because her parents had taken a year's lease on a luxury apartment on Columbus Avenue at Eighty-fourth Street. It would be a convenient walk from there across the park to the doctor's office. The move would be in two weeks' time, on January 1, the start of a new year, and there was a lot to do buying furniture.

We made another plan to get together, but when Louise

turned up that day, we postponed to the following week.

It was Wanda who communicated to me the bad news that Vivyan had been rushed to the hospital. The oncologist had adjusted the medication, but the night after her third injection, Vivyan had awakened with a terrible burning in her throat and a 105-degree fever. She was now in critical condition at Mount Sinai. Between her mother and father and Louise, someone was with her round the clock. Vivyan's sister was flying in from Sweden.

Wanda and I discussed whether we should ask to visit. Circumspectly we inquired and were politely enjoined to stay in touch by phone. So began the vigil of Vivyan's friends, all those people who were in the habit of leaving messages on her machine. We talked to Vivyan's mother or to Louise. We talked to one another. Meanwhile, out of reach of our solicitude, our delirious friend lay muttering phrases in languages no one could decipher.

"No better," said Vivyan's mother on the second day of the crisis and the third. "Still the fever. Still the delirium." On the fourth day, the news was more encouraging. The fever was down a bit, and Vivyan was reported to be more lucid. Vivyan's father, whom I reached at the new apartment, was hopeful she could come home on the weekend.

One friend, Susan, who had traveled out West with Vivyan in emulation of *Thelma and Louise,* did get to visit. Susan had happened to drop by the hospital in an interlude when no one else was available to be at Vivyan's side.

"But I wish I hadn't seen her," she confided to me in our telephone conversation later that evening. "It was the eyes"—her voice quavered. "The eyes in that skeletal face."

Vivyan, as Susan described her, was lucid but intensely restless. She was out of bed and pacing the room, wringing her hands and rubbing her elbows, sitting, standing, pacing. Susan said Vivyan definitely wanted to live, indeed hoped to live. She was looking forward to moving into the new apartment; she talked about its rooms and view and location.

"But she looked so awful, so frightening," said Susan. "You know how thin she was to begin with. Just imagine her twenty or thirty pounds less."

When I called the hospital the next day, Vivyan's mother spoke of an alarming change. Vivyan's blood pressure had dropped, and she was now on a ventilator.

"She's going to die," I announced to the white walls of my apartment, trying to make vivid the realization by saying the words aloud. I had understood that Vivyan might die when I first heard about the recurrence of cancer. We all know that cancer in the liver is supposed to kill you. But Vivyan had been so convincing that hers was a tractable kind. Wanda and I both had believed her when she said it was colon cancer in disguise. Why do these arduous, expensive treatments exist if they cannot effect a cure, if they only make you sicker?

Yes, there it was. Vivyan would die, my peer, my close, dear friend. It struck me she would be the first friend my own age to die whose death would not seem egregiously early, the first about whom one couldn't say, "Oh, but she died so young." I felt a little dizzy and suddenly isolated. For relief, I phoned Wanda.

Wanda said she had never personally known anyone except grandparents to die. She spoke as if she were entitled to be spared such jolting deprivations.

It was Wanda, however, who insisted that Vivyan herself had had premonitions—not in the hospital when she was clinging to life, to the apartment, to sunlight, to future days, but earlier. Wanda recalled that she had talked about it very calmly.

Wanda believed that Vivyan couldn't live without love; yet, she couldn't get love. She had chosen people who couldn't give it to her—Michael with his drinking and depression, Louise with her blandishments and her treachery. Vivyan had at once a tragic and a fatalistic view of life. She had told Wanda that she had been dealt a bad hand.

"Did she really say that?" I asked, intrigued. Then as always, I admired Vivyan's style. Or call it her existential flair. She didn't need to scramble to make things come out right.

"Yes," said Wanda. "Very matter-of-factly. Very calmly."

A day and a night after Vivyan's blood pressure dropped, her heart stopped beating. I learned this from Tom, who answered my morning call to the hospital. Vivyan, he told me, had been revived after nine minutes, but that was too long a lapse for the continued functioning of her brain.

"Will she live?" I asked, not quite understanding.

"Only as a vegetable," said Tom.

The next three days, as Wanda and I heard about them, sounded bitter, dismal, chaotic. Louise wanted to keep Vivyan alive. She observed that when Vivyan was taken off the ventilator, she choked and gasped for air. Surely this showed a clinging to life if not a sign of consciousness. The family opposed Louise and accused her of willful perversity in making a fetish of a living corpse. Yet what should they do? What could they do, given that Vivyan had not signed a living will? I don't know how the legalities finally got resolved, but on the third night, when Louise had left her post to go off and sleep a bit, Tom, as next of kin, signed the permission to stop the life support. Initially, he had been kept away from the crisis. His grandparents had wanted to protect him. Finally, though, he had joined them and his aunt in the sickroom. So it was Vivyan's son, the child she once told me she had first imagined as a twin but then come to see as a mix of son and younger sibling, who took responsibility for her moment of dying.

6

Though Vivyan hadn't been at poker for six months, I wanted the group to know what had happened. I had phoned Leslie when I knew Vivyan was dying, and when she died, I hastened to phone Miriam. It was a few days before a scheduled poker game, though Miriam had not yet made her usual call to confirm my bringing the cheese.

"Do you think I should alert the others in advance of the game?" I asked. "I mean the ones who knew Vivyan—Leslie, Bitsy, and Janice."

"I don't know," Miriam pondered. "Don't forget that this means a great deal more to you than it does to others."

I decided to wait. The game, after all, was just a few days off, our first of the new year. I think I looked to it as a kind of mini memorial. Vivyan's family was organizing no official service, though Wanda and I visited in the starkly furnished Columbus Avenue apartment, with its picture windows facing the park. We listened to Vivyan's mother talk about plans to bury Vivyan's ashes in a little cemetery in Massachusetts, where she and her husband had lived and had friends. The ashes had already been transported there, but now there was a wait, until the spring thaw, before they could be deposited in the earth. Vivyan's sister, next to me on the sofa, talked quietly in French about their special bond. The parents had gone off and traveled when the sisters were little. They had felt abandoned. They had had only each another.

The dramatis personae of Vivyan's life were assuming their postmortem roles. Michael had taken his place as the loyal and devoted friend, helping to sort out bills and insurance. Louise had become the enemy, uniting the family in hate. The latest indignity, said Vivyan's mother, wringing her hands, was the obituary in the *Times*. Wanda and I had seen it too. It had been submitted by Louise, identifying herself as Vivyan's "companion."

"Vivyan would have been aghast," I concurred. "She was the soul of personal discretion."

I knew I wasn't lying, but I wasn't telling the truth either. I was saying, in the face of their terrible pain, what people wanted to hear. And Louise's pain? An image flashed inside me of her desolate defiance. And mine?

Because of my walks with Vivyan and our hunt for the apartment, the whole city served to evoke her. No place did so more than Jane Street, the next street over from Horatio. Parking my car in front of Miriam's apartment, I felt the reverberating emptiness that makes absence into a mournful presence. I rang Miriam's buzzer and, clutching the plastic bag that contained my pound of Brie, I climbed the three flights of stairs to the apartment.

With the banter of greetings and the account of Bitsy's recent trip to Nigeria to see her Tanzanian boyfriend, it wasn't easy to find the opening I sought. Having passed the tofu, as requested, to Miriam on my right, I finally inserted my question.

"Do people know about Vivyan's death?"

"I read the obituary in the *Times*," said Leslie.

"Oh no," said Janice.

"Was she sick?" asked Bitsy.

"Liver cancer," I replied. "But she died from a violent reaction to the chemotherapy. Forty-eight years old."

"Oh liver cancer," said our new member, Lisa. "That's usually fatal. I take it this is a former member of the group."

"Yes," I said, controlling a slight tremor in my voice. "Vivyan. She was my friend. A writer and journalist. She was Swedish." I felt like an envoy from the land of the dead.

"That's too bad," said Lisa.

"Miriam," said Bitsy, after a slight pause, looking away from me, "I learned a couple of new games from one of my graduate students. There's 'baseball' and 'spit-in-the-ocean.'"

"Oh great," said Miriam, clapping her hands in mock glee.

"What are they?" asked Leslie.

"Let's see," said Bitsy. "In spit-in-the-ocean, each player gets dealt four cards. A final card is turned up as everybody's wild fifth card. You bet. Then you can draw—exchanging up to four different cards."

"Do I get this?" asked Lisa. "So with the wild card in the center, everyone has at least a pair?"

"Yes," said Bitsy.

"Far out," said Miriam.

"And what's baseball?" asked Janice.

"A seven-card stud game," said Bitsy. "Threes and nines are wild, and if you get a four, you can ask for an extra card face down."

Miriam looked puzzled.

"Four balls and you walk," said Leslie. The others

laughed. I managed a slight smile. Maybe Vivyan wouldn't have minded.

"Well," said Miriam, reaching for a shuffled deck of cards. "We can see about those later. But let's get started. Ante up."

HERMES

"Do you still have your poker game?" asked Willy, as he persisted with his fine small hands in shredding his paper napkin. We sat in a discreet corner of the lunchroom. Already he had asked after Sarah and Matthew, and I had filled him in with bright anecdotal updates. Matthew was finishing college and, yes, still riding his bike. Sarah had read the book Willy had made such a show of bringing her, but, sad to say, I hadn't.

"Yes," I answered in response to the query about poker. Presumably we were sticking to safe subjects. The effort intensified my sense of danger. I didn't tell him how the poker game had for me lost its carefree innocence. That would have given him too much pleasure.

I remembered all his little jabs about my playing poker. Willy had resented my poker game as he resented most of the activities that filled the pages of my daily organizer: tennis games, recorder trio, dinners with friends. These formed what he saw as an elaborate system of fortifications that existed to keep him at bay. He laid siege. I resisted. Yet hadn't I been the one, as Willy never tired of reminding me, who had initiated the campaign?

"We're still playing." I mustered a fortifying smile. "Once a month."

"Women, of course. Still just women?" He raised the institutional tea cup to his lips. I remembered his small, rather delicate mouth. Mine, we had joked, had been so much bigger than his. He had the sculptor's perceptive eye.

"Of course," I replied, smiling more broadly. "You know that was the idea. A women's poker game. It's fun."

I sipped my tea, wondering if he noticed how some of it had spilled into the saucer. He had come over to my table as I was finishing my lunch and asked if he could join me. The previous week, at one of the large round tables, we had sat together with colleagues. That had gone all right, though I had been irked with myself for choosing the seat right next to him. Just seeing him, and certainly sitting side by side—while noting, dispassionately, that he had lost a bit more hair—I had felt the old rush of excitement. It was as if six years counted for nothing. Throughout that first encounter the week before, we had both been animated and expansive. Together now, just the two of us, our talk was more constrained.

"And Leslie? She's there too?"

"Yes."

"But you're not close anymore?"

"No, we're not close." Though tempted for a moment, I decided not to lie. Leslie and I had struggled to reestablish our friendship—we had even met for a couple of our old Sunday brunches—but the effort had not been successful. Her recent coldness to me at poker had been palpable.

"That's astonishing. Remember how close you were? She was practically your best friend."

He hasn't changed, I thought. It was easier to think about him than about Leslie. It's amazing, but he hasn't changed. Always looking for the weak spot.

"She liked you a lot," I said, remembering his insane jealousy. "She thought you and I had the same kind of charm."

"Hmm." He seemed to be seriously thinking this over. "Perhaps that's true. We had the charm of scoundrels."

I said nothing, trying to decide which, if either of us, was a scoundrel. I had often thought that he was just a small, gentle Jewish boy from Brooklyn, a man of delicate sensibility, easily afraid. In light of this assessment, *his* seeing himself as a scoundrel seemed almost endearing.

"I knew the bike trip would be a disaster," he continued, apparently not wanting to be deflected.

"How did you know that?" I asked, as I marveled at my failure of caution.

"You just had to look at her," he said. "You could tell she wasn't up to it."

He's a creep, I thought, almost uttering the word aloud. Suddenly in the face of his scorn, I was Leslie's most fervent champion.

"The level of difficulty was misrepresented in the brochure," I explained in an even voice. "It was meant to be intermediate. In fact it wasn't. The hills were fierce."

"*You* did it, though," he interrupted.

"Yes," I replied, "but . . . but I had you to get me going." I smiled to suggest irony, though I knew I was stooping to flattery. "I liked it a lot," I said. "I'd do it again."

"Really?"

"Yes. Anytime. I really loved it."

Annoyance flickered in his long-lashed brown eyes, vying at once with some hard-to-fathom discomfort.

"You really hated my going on that trip, didn't you?" I probed.

"Yes," he admitted. "I hated it."

"But that wasn't fair, you know." I felt myself slipping, I had *already* slipped, right back into the thrusts and parries, back into the barely controlled nastiness that spread in us both like an infection.

"I would have loved to go with *you*," I continued. "But how could we? At least you inspired me to sign up for the tour. You know, hearing about your trips with Natalie."

Back then, one of the first indications I had had that he might not be altogether nice was the way he talked about Natalie's crying because she couldn't do the hills.

Natalie was Willy's second wife, an appealing woman—intelligent, kind, and attractive—a few years older than he was. (When Natalie turned fifty, Willy and I were both forty-seven.) In their thirties Natalie and Willy had each been married to someone else, and it was a story that Willy liked to tell of how they had been passionate lovers for seven years before getting free to marry one another. I believe the first thing I had ever heard about Willy was how much he loved his wife. I had thought of recruiting him to be part of a faculty panel on the arts I was organizing for Parents' Day, when a colleague warned me Willy wouldn't come to the college on weekends, because that was the time he spent with his wife. They took wonderful walks—across the Brooklyn Bridge, or from one end of Manhattan to the other. They ate dim sum in Chinatown. At Christmas they went cross-country skiing in Switzerland; in June they went biking in France or England.

I heard more later from Willy himself. Natalie hadn't been much of a biker, but Willy had taken her in hand. When he worked out the route, he tried to keep hills to a minimum and to make the whole thing fun. It sounded fun, more fun perhaps than I had ever had in my life, as I imagined the lovely little inns where they stayed and, even more enviable, the way they curled up together on the grass after lunch, to take a little nap before pushing on another thirty kilometers before dinner.

But Natalie had cried on the hills.

I would have done those hills with alacrity, I had thought at the time, so happy to be with him, riding across the French or English countryside, stopping at the inns, sleeping in the shade of the trees. One year they were in the Lake District. Another year it was Burgundy. But every year, Natalie would be reduced to tears. Or that's what Willy seemed to like to emphasize.

Later I said to him, "You couldn't make me cry." I wasn't then talking about biking. "I don't think any man could make me cry."

2

Willy told me he wanted to extract the *concetto* from the *durezza*. That's what he said as we sat facing one another over tea—the drink was always tea and the time was always daytime. Willy liked best the tea I made for him at my apartment, poured into a mug and sweetened with a dollop of honey. We agreed that our nicest times were those Saturday afternoons when we would lie on my couch, heads at opposite ends, each loosely holding onto the other's feet, occasionally reaching to sip from our mugs on the table, as we listened to *Live from the Met*. Willy had gone with Natalie to hear *Boris Godunov*. He and I listened to it on the Saturday afternoon broadcast.

Now, though, we sat at Eclair on West Seventy-second Street, the down-at-heels, past-its-prime little pastry shop to which Willy had introduced me. "I can meet you for a cup of tea after my recorder lesson," I had said, calculating the time available to fit him in between recorder and dinner. I liked the daring of the moment, when, emerging into the street from Courtly Music Unlimited, I would disengage from Leslie, who played the tenor recorder, and our other friend Mary, who played the alto in our little trio. "No I'm not taking the subway. I'm meeting a friend," I would murmur, and they didn't seem to give it a second thought. While Leslie and Mary disappeared into the station house, I would cross Seventy-second and walk the half block to the restaurant. Dependably, Willy would be waiting out front. I remember him with his hands in the pockets of his brown suede leather jacket, which Natalie had bought him for Christmas. In warmer weather he might be wearing one of his checked short-sleeved shirts, which I liked so much because they reminded me of the shirts boys wore to school in junior high. His shirts made Willy seem innocent, as did his taste in restaurants. At Eclair the pastries had too much cream in them, and the old Russian waiters had spots on their white shirts. For Willy the place had a history. It was where he had trysted with Natalie when they were each married to their previous spouses.

But Willy wanted to extract the *concetto* from the *durezza*. It must have been spring or summer when he said this, for I remember him pulling his reading glasses from the pocket of a checked shirt along with a folded piece of paper. I had leaned back in my chair, expectant, a bit dreamy. There is something so pleasant about the prospect of being read to. Then Willy presented the passage from the journal of Vincenzo di Marma, a quattrocento Florentine whom Willy said belonged to Donatello's inner circle. Vincenzo was explaining his craft, but Willy wanted to make a point about him and me. It hurt my feelings to be pegged as the *durezza*—hard stone. Willy was one of those people adept at calling you names under the guise of some clever analysis.

I braced for worse, though clinging to a scrap of hope about the *concetto*. It seemed that might be the beautiful form to emerge from the block of marble. Didn't the word mean essence or inner concept? For Willy, though, ever relentless, the *concetto* was something to be extracted. It was the wresting from me of some moment of surrender.

After everything between us was over, Willy said that he had waited for something, but it hadn't happened.

3

I was Willy's Circe; he was my Hermes. We lived our different strands of myth. It flattered me when Willy called me a temptress, though the casting seemed wrong. How could I be a temptress when I was still and always ten years old—my secret inner age—the serious dark-eyed girl with a maroon barrette pulling awkward hair to the side, the tomboy of checked flannel shirts and scuffed brown oxfords (cowboy boots were for special occasions)? How could I be Willy's "magnificent woman"? His words, if only momentarily, breathed life into the image of an ample-bodied creature with her full-lipped, ironic smile, tolerant, elusive, able to drive men mad.

Meanwhile, Willy seemed to me light in body and spirit—light like his expensive Italian aluminum yellow bicycle, that fleet reliable courier, which swept him from Brooklyn Heights, where he lived with Natalie, to gambol with me in the soft dappled shadows of Prospect Park.

And I, in my heart of hearts, was Hermes' sidekick, bicycle helmet succeeding cowboy hat. We were pals, youths, ephebes—that was Willy's word, what he had been when he was young, a nostalgic myth of his own exquisite beauty. To me then, he and I seemed ephebes together. We pedaled side by side while Willy recited verses from the poems of W. H. Auden. No faintest cloud of adult consciousness dimmed the sunlight of our idyll. Isn't "adult" implicit in adultery? The naming of our transgression always took me by surprise.

To credit Willy's version, I did pursue him. I looked up the time and place of his class and then "encountered" him in the long half-tiled institutional corridor.

"I was just going to call you," I said. "I hate to ask, but would you be willing to talk about art on Parents' Day?"

He made a wry face. "Yes," he said. "One has to pay one's dues."

"I'm so glad," I said. "I was told you wouldn't do it. But I'm glad my source was wrong. I'll come to your session."

I did, sitting in the front row in my crisp, professional, short-skirted beige spring suit. Next to me was an older woman from Jamaica, whose daughter, she told me, wanted to major in business but loved art. Willy raced through his comparison of Donatello and Michelangelo in a disquisition on their Davids—lithe quattrocento bronze ephebe, seicento marble paragon of muscular manhood. Later he told me he had talked so fast because he had been looking at my legs. He also said he thought I must be nice from the way I talked to the woman at my side.

I phoned Willy at his home in Brooklyn Heights, choosing a time I knew his wife would be at work. I had rehearsed the words of an inviting but casual proposal for him to lunch with me at school. After the call, I ambled into Prospect Park. I had been so nervous about calling, worried he would find me pushy or silly. Now I felt like a cumulus cloud as I billowed to the far side of the Great Meadow. I sat on the ground, stretched out on a gentle hill that was catching the afternoon sun, and fell asleep.

Yes, I started it. Before my own marriage I had had a rule about not being involved with married men. But I never even gave that old prohibition a thought. Did I regret my rashness? I don't think so. For all the waste of spirit, there was a wonderful spark to it all. So if I contemplate regret, it would be hard to say if I regretted getting into the affair in the first place. Or being unable to sustain it. I did, though, very soon feel bad about Natalie. She was so obviously a better person than he was—kinder, more loyal, truly gracious rather than just charming. She also offered him something I knew I could never match. Natalie seemed the kind of woman who could love a man wholeheartedly, who could make him the center of her life. I found myself marveling, even as we two conspired, that he could play so fast and loose with their love. Isn't it odd that one can admire something even when implicated in pulling it down?

I didn't know yet, the day I fell asleep on the hill, that he was as flirtatious as I was. "I don't need to go to bed with a woman," he told me at that first lunch. "I just need to know that she wants to go to bed with me." His words burned hot somewhere in my chest. The rush of fear and detection reminded me of being caught shoplifting.

We moved from the lunch to my bedroom by way of Prospect Park. Willy had been riding in the park and was stopping to do an errand in my neighborhood. When he saw me, he got off his bike, and we stood together on the sidewalk. His small hands rested lightly on the black handlebars. I gazed at the curve of his chest beneath his V-neck shirt, tucked so neatly into his biking shorts. The shorts and shirt were both a tasteful solid black. He explained that serious bikers shave their legs to cut down on wind resistance.

Willy said he loved to encourage people to bike. He said he could do his own nine laps and then meet me at the end of his real workout.

The date was enough of a secret for me to conceal it from Leslie when we had our brunch that Sunday in Manhattan. I kept a furtive eye on the time as she and I were finishing our second cup of tea, then drove back in a hurry over the Brooklyn Bridge.

Following Willy's instructions, I turned clockwise inside the Third Street entrance to the park and started slowly pedaling against the flow of bikers—this had been Willy's suggestion to ensure that we would meet. I hadn't yet bought my good Cannondale touring bike, which later he came with me to select. So there I was on an old borrowed five-speed Peugeot, the amateur in ordinary shorts and a T-shirt, as the pros whizzed past me—swift, sleek, helmeted, blurred. Anxiety knotted in my chest. I was sure I would miss him. Then, with a little happy start of recognition, I sighted him, standing from his seat, rhythmically pushing the pedals, as he came up the long north-side hill.

I did the hill with him twice that day, the second time so short of breath I couldn't speak. "It will get easier," he said. "The only way you can improve is if you push on the hills." That was the day, on the parts of the ride when I had breath to talk, on which I told him of my love for women.

I spoke to him about Laura, my married friend who lived

in Virginia. "I'll wait for her until she's seventy," I told Willy.
I felt heroic saying that, entranced with my own fidelity as
much as with Laura herself. By the time Laura was seventy,
I figured she would either have divorced her corporate
lawyer husband or he would have died. We would live
together with children and grandchildren around us. Willy
wanted to have me respond to him the way I did to Laura.
That was the *concetto* to be extracted from the *durezza*.

It excited Willy to hear about my loving Laura. And she
too, as I talked to her in our long-distance calls, liked to hear
about Willy. "Does he look cute in his biking shorts?" she
asked. He gave me a picture of himself as a young man,
working shirtless out of doors the summer he had gone digging in Turkey. I sent it to Laura and she pinned it to a shelf
in a discreet corner of her study.

After he became my lover, Willy bought me a set of 250-
thread-count percale cotton sheets because the ones Laura
had sent me from L. L. Bean were wearing out.

Once Sarah came home early from college when he was
still in my room, lying like a supine sculptor's model on his
sheets. I came out from the bedroom, securing the sash of
my green silk bathrobe.

"Could you take a walk for half an hour?" I asked her,
sheepishly raising my eyebrows.

"Why?" she said. "It doesn't embarrass *me*."

"But it does me," I retorted.

"You have to dress and leave," I told Willy when she had gone out.

"Why?" he asked.

In some way, I was always glad to have him leave. I would close the door behind him and turn with relief to some small task. Willy got irritated when I spoke of our false position, for surely I had known what our situation would be. I would try to explain that I hadn't known what it would *feel* like. The dreariness of an adulterous liaison. The envy of the social and public sphere in which he moved with his wife and to which I was so conscious that he returned when he left my bed. Or am I just fixing on excuses? I've been told by more men than one that I'm like a man when sex is over. I want to get up and do my chores or return my telephone calls. A terrible impatience comes upon me. Call it *la durezza* if you like. Yet whenever Willy left, even when it was I who had urged him to go, I was also sorry.

The last time Willy and I ever made love was on a night Natalie was out of town. It was raining, so Willy came to Park Slope on the train to meet me for dinner. We met at a restaurant, because, officially, our affair had ended. Over dessert, with his best boyish flourish, Willy whipped out his toothbrush. "I'm prepared," he announced.

"You can come home with me," I conceded, "but I don't want you to stay overnight."

"All or nothing," said Willy.

In the end we did it my way. I look back to that night as

passionate, even tender, but still I made him leave. Unfortunately the subway was running with delays. I'm sure Willy felt raw, standing on the dreary platform at two in the morning, while I lay in my bed with the nice sheets.

4

When I think of Willy and me at our best, I see us in the park. We did our laps. I extended to six, as Willy cajoled me through the last two circuits. "Let's do another," he said after our usual four. "And now just one more." I was too proud and too eager to say no. And then I had ridden twenty miles.

Sometimes when the weather was nice and he didn't have to go home right away, we would lie on the grass after biking and feel the rays of the late afternoon sun on our faces. The bikes would lie carefully positioned on their sides a few feet off, our helmets serving as our head rests. "You're the right size for me," said Willy, as I nestled alongside him in the crook of his arm. One day he took off his shoes and socks, but then later told me he had been embarrassed by my looking at his naked feet. He said this as if his embarrassment were my fault. Did I say something about the little tufts of hair on his toes? People's feet can be surprising. One is so quickly aware of hands, but there's a nakedness about feet, an exposure. I do remember thinking these were a man's feet, even though they were quite slender and delicate. When we lay in my apartment on the sofa, Willy usually kept on his socks.

Biking ended in November, at least the two falls we were together, and then the park drew us as a place to walk. As a boy Willy had gone with his mother to the duck pond. I heard about her, so many years a widow, so talented a pianist, and about his dead father and his sister and brother, without ever meeting any of them. Or we would talk about the park itself, the park that Willy said was the one Frederick Law Olmsted had done right. Willy would point out this and that. I do love being with people who help me to see the things around me more clearly.

One late November afternoon we were walking in Prospect Park as usual. In the waning afternoon light, we had lingered at the duck pond and then sat on a grassy knoll. We had even roughhoused a little amid the swirling fallen leaves. In the distance an old woman, heavyset and with wild long gray hair under a biking helmet, was walking her bicycle over the grass. "I know that woman," said Willy. "Believe it or not, she used to be very beautiful."

The sun was going down. Suddenly the air had a sharp chill. Willy said he needed to get home to Natalie. We started to make our way out of the park.

I'm not sure why I reached into my jacket pocket to clutch my house keys, but I remember my pride in not panicking when they weren't there.

"I must have dropped them," I said to Willy, still impressed with my capacity for calm. "Maybe it was when we were sitting or playing."

"Let's look," he said.

"I know you need to get home."

"Never mind. Let's look."

We walked back to the knoll where we had been sitting, then walked down to the spot where we had tumbled in the grass. Not finding the keys in these obvious places, we fanned out to cover more ground. Willy became the archeologist directing a delicate excavation. I tried to keep my eyes on the grass and not think about the hours ahead, how I would wait on my stoop in the evening chill for one of the other occupants of my brownstone to return and open the front door, then call a locksmith to force the door to my own apartment.

"If the keys are lost, never mind," I said to Willy. "I'll manage."

We were close to giving up when we both looked up. Across the field, a hundred yards away from us, the old lady with the bicycle was dangling something in her exuberantly raised hand.

"I'm a great finder of things," she said when we went up to her. "I have special powers."

Willy and I thanked her and then walked away, intimate in our conspiracy of relief. We were pleased with ourselves that we had both behaved so well. "I wouldn't have abandoned you," said Willy.

"But you could have," I said.

"Yes, it would have been dicey for me," said Willy, "but

I wouldn't have left you until you got into your house."

I wondered if I were at all sorry the keys had been found.

5

The affair ended badly. There was a silly dinner when Laura came to town, and Willy, Natalie, Laura, and I sat boxed together eating couscous at the Moroccan Star on Atlantic Avenue. Willy and Laura flirted—she drew him out about his craft as a sculptor—while Natalie and I, after a few polite exchanges, were relieved to sit more or less silent through the ordeal. I remember having a big fight with Willy afterward, because he said he had sat in the restaurant wanting to kiss Laura's mouth.

At that point, Willy and I were trying to be just friends. I like to think that, belatedly, I had come to my moral and rational senses. I was also in the grip of a familiar numbness that made it impossible for me to sustain a sexual liaison. In an old recurrent dream, a menacing man, who shot me or squirted me with a hose, had now taken on Willy's face. Armed with pistols, he searched for me amid urban rubble. I cowered from his attack behind a pile of jagged stones. To appease my conscience *and* escape the nightmares, I had broken off sex. But then there was the backsliding of the dinner with the toothbrush, which, in turn, led to the pregnancy scare, which itself turned out to be just the onset of menopause. When Willy behaved execrably about "the baby"—the putative creature whom I, at forty-eight, was thinking of raising on my own and had taken to calling Alexander—Laura took down Willy's picture from her study.

6

When Willy and Natalie separated, I learned about it third- or fourth-hand. Colleagues at school expressed surprise, because Willy and Natalie had seemed such a perfect couple. But then, knowing Willy, so charming and so flawed, they were not surprised at all. Most of the gossipers didn't know about Willy and me, or if they did, they pretended not to. The report was that Willy had a new girlfriend—someone young. I had heard all this before Willy and I met in the lunchroom. We had hardly spoken to one another in four years.

During one of our lunches that spring—we must have been on the same schedule to run into one another with such regularity—I broached the subject of Natalie.

"Do you see her?" I asked.

"Yes," he said, "A little. But we're not really friends. I made a terrible mistake." His look into my eyes was pointedly rueful but short of a reproach.

"And your new friend?" I asked, warding off even the hint of an opportunity for Willy to voice his theory that it was I who had ruined his life.

"She's a funny little thing," said Willy. They had lived together for a while but weren't doing so now. Willy complained, in a way that was also a small boast, how he had had to do all the cooking.

I heard more when he came to my new apartment for tea. We had both moved to new addresses in Manhattan, I to do something cheering and different with my kids gone, he to live apart from Natalie. My place was on the Upper West Side, his on the Upper East, so I had invited him over. I must have been prompted by chagrin when he saw me hobbling with a stiff Achilles tendon and remarked on my gait. I think I invited him over because I missed his old response to me. I hated it when he asked me if I'd gone through menopause.

As I stood at the counter at Eclair, now the nearest pastry shop to my new apartment, selecting an assortment of cakes and tarts, as usual all too full of cream, to take home to serve with the tea, I was expectant and a little giddy. By the time Willy and I were onto our third cup of Earl Grey, this one laced with bourbon, I knew my folly.

His girlfriend wanted to have a baby. Willy made a wry face to accompany this communication. He presented himself as a weary ghost trailing through his life's debris. "I threw away happiness," he said. He was aware of time passing, of his own attractiveness being subject to time. "I'm fifty-three," he said. "At a certain point, one loses it." In the evenings he would drink Scotch and read—a gesture of loyalty to Natalie who loved to read—and sometimes laugh and cry out loud. Of course, he was still biking, though we had never crossed paths when I went to ride in Central Park with my Cannondale, the bike he had helped me pick out. Maybe it was just as well. Willy told me that he biked every evening with his girlfriend. Her name was Lisa, and she was thirty-two. "And," he added, smiling more to himself than at me, "you should see her do the hills!"

7

I have never told Willy about my being thrown out of the poker game. It may seem odd, given all I know about him, that I can still imagine telling him. I always liked his wit, with its power to transform a gruesome experience into something funny and harmless. I didn't tell him, though, and won't. I still don't trust him. Also, our contact is less— both less frequent and less charged. Willy declares that he is in love, really in love, with an art historian who lives and works in Vienna. She's forty-four to his fifty-six. I assume she's premenopausal. I have no idea if she's a biker.

The letter from Leslie arrived that very day three years ago when Willy came over for tea, the day I half hoped to rekindle our affair. Or at least to give it one last coda. After Willy left my apartment, I changed into old clothes, scraped and washed the dishes, and felt morosely absorbed in the aftertaste of my own thwarted vanity. For something else to do, I drifted down to the mailboxes in the lobby. It's so rare to get a real letter these days, not a bill or solicitation or promotion, that I was interested to see the hand-addressed envelope, though I wondered at Leslie's name on it as the sender.

Back in my apartment, I sat down with the letter on the couch, opened it, and pulled out the handwritten page.

There were no words of conventional greeting or sign off, just our two names, mine at the top of the page and hers at the bottom, positioned like opposing queens on a chessboard or boxers in opposite corners of a ring. I had to read two or three sentences before understanding that this was something really bad.

> *Jenny,*
>
> *For some time now, our friendship has been a thing of the past. I had hoped that time would ease my feelings, but it really hasn't. The strain and tension I experience in your company has infected my pleasure in the poker game. I thought that the number of people playing poker would dilute and assuage my feelings, but unfortunately it has not.*
>
> *As you know I dropped out of the recorder trio to leave it to you, but I will not give up poker. I have thought a lot about this and have talked it over with Miriam. Since my feelings are not going to change, the only solution is for you to stop coming to the game. Miriam backs me in this resolution.*
>
> *I am sorry to cause you hurt, but I am unwilling to bear it myself.*
>
> *I hope things go well with you.*
>
> *Leslie*

That night I cried long and hard into my pillow, muffling the sound by pulling the pillow around my ears. The searing letter lay buried in the bottom of the drawer where, angry and ashamed, I had stuffed it. Across Central Park perhaps Willy sat with his book and his Scotch, laughing and crying over life and literature. Can I be certain that my tears were not the slightest bit for him and his not at all for me?

HOUSE OF CARDS

*T*he story of my last months in the poker game begins with talk of penises.

"Did you see the piece in *The New Yorker* about the giant penis?" asked Miriam one early summer evening as we were getting ready to count out the chips.

"No," I said, seconded by Bitsy and Lisa, our new member who worked in banking. Why am I someone, I wondered, who is never in the know about a giant penis?

"It's in the Terrence McNally play," Miriam explained. "This guy is lying about on the stage. And then he stands up."

"And he's really huge!" prompted Leslie, at poker that evening wearing her THELMA AND LOUISE FINISHING SCHOOL T-shirt. "So this guy's on stage with a huge dick?"

"Yes," said Miriam.

"I'm going to see the play tomorrow!" said Leslie. "I always go to plays with frontal nudity."

Terrence McNally's giant penis set Leslie to musing. "I was with a man once. We had taken off our clothes. And he was this big unerect." Leslie spread her hands at least eight inches. "He said it was a real problem for him," she continued.

"Like a woman with breasts too large," offered Bitsy.

"Yes, but a woman could have something done about it," said Janice.

"I want to hear about Leslie," interjected Miriam. "What happened?"

"We ended up not having sex."

"Because of the dick?" asked Terry, Leslie's good friend, a children's book illustrator and now a poker regular.

"I didn't really like him enough."

"But you had taken off your clothes," I said.

"In those days I took off my clothes for everyone."

"Hmm," mimicked Miriam, "now that we're naked, let's see if I like you."

"Let's play poker," I suggested, when the laughter finally abated.

"Okay," said Miriam. "Let's draw for who's going to deal."

As I think back, I'm pretty sure I never told a penis joke. That just wasn't my mode. It was Miriam and Leslie, the two who shared a delight in cards and T-shirts, logos and wacky puns, who were also the penis joke champions, awesome in their repertoire and range.

"Miriam, how was your trip to Senegal?" asked Bitsy, at the start of another evening.

"Great!" said Miriam. "I went to a wild game preserve. There are all kinds of wonderful animals. And you can walk around. I saw wild boars."

"Aren't you afraid they'll attack you?" asked Janice.

"They don't really want to be with you," explained Miriam. "They want to be with one another."

"That's good," I chimed in.

"I was somewhere once," said Miriam, "where there was a boar. I kept looking at it. And I called my friends and said, 'That boar has its intestines hanging out.' They came up to me and laughed."

"Why?" asked Janice.

"They said, 'That's not his intestines. That's his penis.'"

"What's a wild boar's penis like?" asked Leslie.

"It's like little corkscrew curls," explained Miriam. "And it goes on and on."

I laughed along with the others but with an undercurrent of uneasiness, my private knowledge that I was pretending. Miriam's story was humorous, but I was laughing mainly to be part of the group. Eager to seem knowing and casual, I did my best to look amused and laugh on cue, masking my sense of feeling different.

I don't mean to suggest that, in contrast with the others, I was puritanical. That wasn't it. The difference was more a question of language, of style. I'd always liked penises, at least liked them all right, *and* sometimes they had scared me. But either way, I'd never known how to joke or boast about them. Or to be crude. Back when I was in my teens, a friend had told me that the boy dancing with her had had "a hard-on." Her blunt words, not the fact of the erection, shocked me. Perhaps I'd been too focused on my reading of nineteenth-century novels. Dickens and Dostoevsky didn't talk about hard-ons. I also had read *Marjorie Morningstar* and *Goodbye, Columbus*—weren't there penises in these?— but I was profoundly reticent. I didn't talk about sex to my friends, and during sex . . . I guess I'd have to say I kept quiet. It pleased me that a man had once called me a "sexual buc-caneer," but whatever I did that led him to this formulation, it wasn't verbal lewdness. One time, almost as an experi-ment, I tried to improvise. "It's so big," I said. "Oh, it's so big." I heard my breathy utterance. It seemed to float above the bed where the man and I lay touching and gasping. Are those really my words? I wondered.

It's not that I couldn't match Leslie's or Miriam's sexual past penis for penis. When I last updated my list, I'd gone to bed with twenty-one men—most of these during the time when *I* took off my clothes a lot—and eleven women. I'd say that was a long enough list to earn me my credentials as a member of the sexual-revolution generation. And it didn't even include the men I'd played at sex with without having penetration. These numbers, however, told nothing of how I had felt. Fondling one penis or another, I'd been excited but generally uneasy—worried, in the final analysis, that the penises would go off, sort of like firecrackers. And when they did . . . well once, when I was still a virgin, and Roger Heron, making out with me in his college dorm room, lost control and came all over my stomach, I nearly threw up. Roger apologized profusely. In later years, I often thought of his apology and wished I hadn't made him feel ashamed.

I got better at coping with male orgasms. When I was married, it was vastly easier. I felt more trust. Also, between wanting babies and using birth control, I didn't have to *see* the semen. That made a big difference to me. It was seeing it and, even more, feeling it on my skin that bothered me. I've never liked anything viscous, not even suntan lotion. Part of my relief in being with women was in not having to cope with shooting semen, and the thought of all those little sperm swimming around in it. Strangely, women's fluids didn't bother me. Yet at the same time I missed the penises—*and* the men who went with them.

No one else in the poker group had any experience with women. No one in the poker game would have even called herself bisexual, at least not once Vivyan was gone. As now I look back, I think this caused me to feel that I was always hiding something.

If you asked Miriam why her feelings for me changed, I'm sure, if she could still remember, she'd never think even to mention my sexuality. Her younger sister, Gina, was a lesbian. Once at poker Miriam told about Gina's coming over with her girlfriend. She laughingly described Gina and the girlfriend cooing and holding hands, that in-your-face public display of affection—PDA, my daughter calls it—which discreet people generally abhor. Miriam was very funny, as she could invariably be when she got on a riff, but I couldn't help wondering if a hetero couple would have inspired the same hilarity. I'm sure this question never troubled Miriam. I'm equally sure she didn't worry a jot about me and the possibility of offending me. No, Miriam would never have thought it mattered that I was . . . well, whatever I was. If you were to ask Miriam what had happened between us, my guess is that *she* would have talked about the cheating, about Alice, and maybe about the cheese.

2

The hand in question was a showdown between me and Miriam. "Let's play seven-card high-low, deuces wild and rolling," I announced, when it was my turn to deal. This was the game Vivyan had taught us—I'm sure no one else remembered that, but in memory of her, I often chose it.

"What's rolling?" asked Lisa. "Remind me."

Someone always forgot, and I'd carefully explain the game.

"Deuces are wild," I said, "and after a deuce is dealt up, the next up card, say, a six, is wild as well. But then if another deuce shows, it's the card after that that's wild and no longer the six."

"So you always have two wild cards," added Miriam, to complete the explanation. "At least if deuces show."

"Everyone ready?" I asked. I tried to imitate Leslie's patter as, a little awkwardly, I flung out the cards to the seven players, including myself, around the table. I just never could get that right flick of the wrist, and the whole procedure took my utmost concentration. "A two for you. Ah, there's a wild card," I said to Lisa on my left. "Ah, lucky eights," I said to Leslie, next to her. "Now twos and eights are wild. Oh, a royal queen," I said to Bitsy. "Working on a royal flush."

Despite my jaunty banter, no one seemed to be getting anything good, except perhaps Miriam, whose bold raises started scaring people off. "I fold," said Leslie, followed in short order by Bitsy. "Too rich for me," said Janice. "Me too," said Terry, and then Lisa. If I hadn't been so entangled in dealing—worrying about my small motor coordination while trying to display a little panache, I might have folded as well. I'd stayed in, thinking I might have a decent low with a hidden wild eight usable as an ace or deuce, but then jacks rather than eights were wild, and my final card down, a second three, totally ruined my hand. By the time I dealt that final card down, Miriam and I were the only ones who hadn't folded. I still had the option to fold, but I didn't want to. I'd put in so many chips, blue and red ones as well as whites, why not persist through just one more round of betting? Folding, I'd lose everything. Staying in and second-guessing Miriam on the high-low call, I had a chance to split the pot

with her. I bet a red chip worth fifty cents; Miriam put in a
blue, raising the bet to a dollar. Nervously I matched her,
taking back my red and flipping in a blue in its place. I wondered what she had.

Miriam was showing an ace and a queen—both spades—
and a pair of fives; I, a ten, a three, and a pair of sevens.
Jacks, which neither of us had face up, were still the second
wild card in addition to deuces.

Should I go for high or low? My low would show a ten
high—that was weak. But if I decided to go instead for high,
I'd have to rely on two pairs—of threes and sevens. Either
way, I was vulnerable. My only real chance was to declare the
opposite of Miriam. But what would she do?

If Miriam chose to use her ace and one of the fives, she
had the makings of a good low. On the other hand, she
could equally well have a high. She could have three fives; it
was possible she had a flush. Even four of a kind wasn't out
of the question. She might easily be concealing wild cards,
as, of course, might I, but I wasn't. I think if I'd focused less
on what Miriam had showing and more on what *my* cards
might mean to her, I might have been more coolheaded and
strategic. Sadly, I was too busy worrying about Miriam's
hand to consider how she might read mine. Isn't one secret
of good poker play sensing the other players' vulnerability as
well as your own? After all, Miriam, too, would want us to
declare in different ways.

"Wait a minute," I said, desperate for more time. "I'm thinking." I was almost ready to conclude that Miriam would declare for low, so I should go for high. But then, worrying I had only the two lowish pairs and Miriam could easily have two higher pairs or three of a kind, my going high seemed awfully risky. Better call low, I thought. Meanwhile, Leslie was doing her routine. "Remember, it's just like a thermometer. Red for high, blue for low. Are you ready? One, two, three."

Right on three, Miriam opened her hand to show a blue chip on her palm. I was a beat behind her, still lost in indecision, a blue chip in my left hand and a red in the right. I heard the "one, two, three." I had my left fist forward, but then I vacillated, pulling that hand back and opening my right instead to show the red.

"You've really got to open at the same time," said Lisa.

"Yes, people get shot for that," said Terry.

Leslie said nothing.

I looked up quizzically. "Would you like . . . ?" I trailed off.

"You seemed to be changing your mind," said Miriam.

"No, that's what I was going to do," I mumbled, as I raked in my half of the chips. There were a lot of them, because Miriam had forced a big increase in the pot.

For the rest of the evening I looked desperately for another chance to be the first to open my hand on a high-low call. But we had only two more high-low declarations, and in both instances I had already folded. On one of them Miriam jokingly pulled back her hand and did a mock switch. I was mortified.

What I had wanted to say was, "You take the whole pot. I messed up." But I was too embarrassed to suggest that I might have seen Miriam's chip before deciding on mine.

In therapy I spent a whole session talking about what had happened. My shrink said, "You need to tell one person in the group what you've just told me."

"That's a good idea," I said, and wondered if it should be Bitsy or Janice. Both were women it seemed possible for me to talk to, and neither had joined in the reproof.

3

My relationship with Miriam was on a downward spiral, if relationship is the word for what we had. Miriam had never been a close friend. She was someone I rarely saw or spoke to outside of poker. Yet we had liked one another and had enjoyed an unself-conscious rapport. I had always looked forward to going to her loft for the poker games, hearing her latest jokes, marveling at the always amusing accounts of her trips to Senegal, Alaska, and other far-flung places. She and Leslie and I had founded the poker game and had played together for six years. We had all been forty-seven when we started, and now we were fifty-three. We had been together the night Operation Desert Storm was launched, and after the game, we had sat on Miriam's bed to watch the broadcast reports of the bombing, finding at least a little solace in being depressed all together. We had played through a Bush–Clinton–Ross Perot debate—the one other night at poker we had ever kept on the television. Moments like these accumulated to form our shared history.

Now, though, when I mounted the stairs to Miriam's loft and met her at the door, I felt anxious. I braced to encounter her. Her hellos seemed cool, her hugs perfunctory, and then we didn't even hug anymore. I knew why Leslie and I weren't friends any longer, but this was more baffling. I wondered if the cause was Miriam's friendship with Leslie. Yet Miriam had made such an obvious effort—and that had been three and a half years back—not to get involved in the fallout from the disastrous bike trip. The way you try not to take sides in a divorce, so as to retain both people as your friends. I might add that I've noticed how hard it is to succeed at this. Is it ever possible to stay equal friends with two people who feel betrayed by one another?

It may be coincidental, but I link Miriam's coolness to me to the period of her spectacular diet. In the last year and a half I played in the poker game, Miriam lost over a hundred pounds.

I first noticed a change in Miriam's appearance when she, her husband, Neil, and I found ourselves together at a birthday party held for Neil's ninety-year-old aunt, Alice Harding. Alice, who had been a well-known theatrical agent, provided a connection between Miriam and me that extended beyond the poker game. She and my mother had been beautiful women together in New York in the thirties and forties and had remained friends to the end of my mother's life. It was visiting Alice with my mother when I was a senior in high school that I had met Neil and his brother, David. Miriam and I were now about the age my mother and Alice had been when I used to go to Alice's house, hoping to see her gorgeous nephews. We sat with a worn-looking Neil on the patio of a Connecticut mansion—home of one of Alice's rich friends—gazing out at the well-tended lawn, bordered with blue hydrangeas, in the soft light of late afternoon. Waiters carried around delicate hors d'oeuvres. "No thank you," said Miriam to the young woman passing the little crab cakes. I complimented Miriam on her weight loss. "Yes, twenty-two pounds," she said and gleefully clapped her hands. She was excited to be buying new clothes.

I think about that day because it is the last nice time I remember having with Miriam. We shared an experience, and had we remained on friendly terms, we might have remembered it together twenty years later.

Alice, at ninety, had that translucent beauty of the very old. She had always been beautiful, right into her fifties and sixties, but at ninety she was extraordinary. She sat with her hands folded softly in her lap and a serene, restrained, almost radiant expression on her face, listening to the flurry of toasts that extolled her beauty. When they concluded, she rose, leaning on her cane.

"Thank you," she said, standing before us. "I'm listening to the things people are saying about me, and do you know what I'm thinking . . . ?" Alice paused for effect. "I'm thinking of my stepmother," she continued. "'Alice,' my stepmother said to me—I must have been sixteen—'you're not beautiful, so you just have to try harder and be better than everybody else.' And I'm thinking . . ." Alice had an intense faraway look on her face. "If she could be here today and hear these things being said to honor me, what would she say?"

"It's amazing," I whispered to Miriam sitting next to me. "She hasn't forgotten anything."

"Or forgiven," Miriam murmured.

Alice stood on that patio, at once in our midst and in the grip of memory, ready, three-quarters of a century after the fact, to confront her stepmother—and to vanquish her.

A year and a half after this milestone occasion, Alice was doing poorly, and Miriam had lost a 110 pounds. Several times a week she went to Weight Watchers or Overeaters Anonymous. She ate mostly salads, and she swam everyday. Her size-eight swimsuit hung over the shower curtain railing in the bathroom of her loft. I marveled at its tininess when I went in there.

"I don't have breasts anymore," Miriam announced to us at the poker table. "I have tit sacks."

She turned to me on her left.

"Alice is in the hospital," she said. "She fell on her head and perhaps also had a stroke."

I thought about Alice, a tough career woman, whose one regret, or so she told me during the lunch we had after my mother died, was that she had never truly loved anyone. Alice had been a poker player. She played in her group—I think it was also a group of women—until she was over ninety. Our group had considered inviting her to visit our game, but then we worried that she might find our stakes too low and that we might find her too difficult. Once Miriam had brought in some beautiful cards with an art deco design for us to play with. She said Alice had given her these cards.

Miriam saw a lot of Alice and felt responsible for her. I wondered if Miriam resented that I didn't have to take care of Alice and she felt that she did. Might I not then have seemed to her the person who hadn't taken care of Leslie and didn't get involved with Alice either? A selfish, callous person, then later, for good measure, also a cheater at poker. I built the case against myself and felt maligned, guilty, and depressed.

"Does Alice still go about?" I asked. "I mean, has she up until now?"

"She's been going out only in a wheelchair," Miriam said. "Just last week we took her to a movie and asked her how she liked it."

Alice had said, "I hate it." "Let's leave her here," Miriam had said to Neil in Alice's hearing. "Then," Miriam said, with a laugh to us at the poker table, "we all got out our aggression and could have a good time."

Losing all that weight should have made Miriam happier. Maybe it did. But it also seemed to make her edgy. It's too tidy to suggest some connection between Miriam's weight loss and a rivalry with me, to suggest that somehow losing the weight made her more avid, more competitive. Henry James urged the would-be writer to be a person on whom nothing is lost. I've always taken that advice to heart. In this case, however, I observed everything and understood very little.

All I can speak of with certainly is chronology. It was around the time Miriam, though no longer dieting, was working vigilantly to maintain her new body that we had our little tension over the cheese.

"Bring something else," Miriam said to me in our phone conversation confirming the date of the next game. "That cheese isn't going." Perhaps she was annoyed to have the left-over cheese in her refrigerator when she was eating only tofu and salads. I could understand why she wouldn't want it around.

"What should I bring?" I asked, trying to disregard the harsh edge in Miriam's voice.

"Surprise us," said Miriam. "Lobster salad. What you will."

"Don't people like cheese?" I asked.

"Well, one time it could be cheese," said Miriam—I felt I was being talked to as if I were an imbecile—"and another time lobster salad."

Anxious to propitiate Miriam and make an appropriate contribution, I went to Zabar's, where I stood a long time gazing at the shelf of fish salads and finally, with agonized self-doubt, chose shrimp. It seemed too literal to get lobster, but shrimp was as far as I dared to deviate from Miriam's suggestion. What a fool I seemed to myself never to have varied from cheese. For six years, I'd brought cheese to the poker game, usually Brie, sometimes Cheddar or Saga Blue or Jarlsburg. I'd never considered anything else. How boring, how unimaginative. Yet bringing cheese had always made me happy.

In Miriam's loft I asked for a plate and, without saying much to anyone, put out my shrimp salad and took my seat.

"Where's the Brie?" asked Bitsy innocently, stopping to notice its absence in the middle of telling us about her recent field trip to Papua New Guinea. Men in the village in which she was staying had murdered two men from a neighboring village and kept waiting for reprisals. She had slept in her mud hut with a machete at her side but wouldn't have known how to use it. Her only food had been bananas, papayas, and pineapples, and lots of cooked greens. The children of the village ate live worms.

"Oh," I said, "do people like the cheese?"

"Oh yes," said Bitsy.

"And Brie?" I asked.

"It's great," said Janice.

"I guess I'll go back to Brie," I said, not looking at Miriam.

That same evening of the cheese discussion, there was

another contretemps over cards. We were playing Black Maria, in which you divide the pot between the highest hand and the highest spade in the hole.

"I guess I have the highest spade in the hole," I said, pulling out my jack of spades, after it was clear Miriam had the highest hand.

"That's not fair," said Miriam. "You were going for high."

"Do you have to say in advance what you're going for?" I asked. "We didn't say that. Don't cards speak?"

"Dealer's call," said Leslie.

"You have to declare in advance," said Terry the dealer.

"Fine," I said, relieved to back off, but embarrassed once again to run aground of protocol.

4

I decided to talk to Janice, whom I'd gotten to know just a little. She had been quiet when she first joined the poker game, but lately she had grown more expansive. One evening, with a toss of her Veronica Lake blond hair, she mentioned an ex-husband.

"I didn't know you'd been married," I said. I had always imagined Janice to have lovers. I saw them as handsome, dark-haired, slightly graying men in their forties, men who still looked good in blue jeans. Perhaps they were cads.

"Yes," she said. "For four and a half years. About ten years ago." Janice made a face.

"You don't miss it!" laughed Leslie.

"No," said Janice. "Who would want to get *married*?"

"The way you say it," said Miriam, grimacing. "*Married!* Who'd want to do that?"

"You didn't like it?" I asked her.

"No," she said. "All that negotiating. So confining."

A couple of months later, one of the two or three times in six years that we played somewhere other than at Miriam's—and consequently got to eat meat—Janice and I left together from the game, going down together in the elevator. Waiting for Janice by the door of the building was a handsome black man with a close-trimmed beard. Perhaps he was around forty. He was wearing jeans. "This is Tony," Janice said to me. I watched them go off hand in hand.

I took the next possible occasion to speak to her about my concerns. It was the end of the next game, back at Miriam's. Together we descended Miriam's staircase and then lingered in the street talking about poker. I said one had to think of new games to keep it interesting. Or new strategies, and we talked about bluffing. Leslie had had a round of anaconda in which she started betting high. She had two kings showing and two sevens. I had a full house, queens high, but I knew Leslie could beat me if she had a full house kings high. She might even have four kings, since we had added a wild card.

I had folded, but Janice thought Leslie might have been bluffing, since in our cautious crowd, it was unusual to bet so high.

"That's what you try to do," said Janice. "Bet high and make the others drop out."

"You know," I said, "I'd like to say something to you. There was a hand a few months ago where I was late opening my fist, and it may have looked like I changed my mind. What I'm not sure of is whether or not I cheated. I was vacillating. But I'm not sure if I saw Miriam's chip before I decided to open my fist with the red. I should have given Miriam the whole pot. That's what I should have done."

"Don't worry," said Janice. "It was a bit strange. But we've all been playing together a long time. Anyone can get mixed up."

"Thank you," I said. "I'm glad I talked to you."

"See you next month," said Janice.

5

I didn't see Janice the next month. I was sick with bronchitis and called Miriam to say I wouldn't be coming to the game. When I had made the call, I felt relieved. I wouldn't have to face the grinding unfriendliness, which, frankly, was beginning to demoralize me. I realized this was the first game I had missed in six years, and at that thought, the air in my apartment seemed eerily still. Maybe I'd never go back. I'd leave altogether, withdrawing with the shreds of a little dignity. A life without poker stretched before me: no straights and flushes, no shopping for the cheese, no penis jokes, no monthly something to look forward to. The dreariness was palpable. I couldn't bear it. It was easier to believe that the situation would improve, that somehow Miriam would like me again and the downward course would get reversed. Then a week before the next scheduled game, I received Leslie's letter, and the choice of staying or leaving was taken away from me. I considered making some response but couldn't think what it should be. A letter? A phone call. To whom? Saying what?

I have never seen Bitsy, Lisa, or Terry again. Nor Miriam. I've not seen her. Nor did she ever call me. About a year ago I read Alice's obituary in the *New York Times*. It did not mention Neil as her next of kin, because he had predeceased his aunt. Walking one day with Miriam to the subway, he dropped dead, without warning, of a heart attack. He was only fifty-eight. I had heard all this from a friend of mine who knows Miriam. I also heard, from the same source, about six months later, that Miriam, still thin, had fallen passionately in love with someone new. My friend said Miriam was deliriously happy. I said, "That's great for Miriam."

Leslie, I encounter occasionally at work, and we both maintain a scrupulous politeness. The first time I saw her, about to cross paths with me on campus, my heart pounded and I felt very bad. I wanted to turn away without speaking, but instead I met up with her and said hello. I decided it was important to master my feelings, and that's what I have done—for the four intervening years.

Then a couple of months ago, I ran into Janice at the Brooklyn Academy of Music. We were both attending one of those early operas that BAM specializes in mounting, events at which you usually see at least ten Manhattanites of your acquaintance. The performance that evening was Monteverdi's *Orfeo,* a marvelously moving piece that ends with Orfeo wandering the earth, an outcast from heaven and hell. Entering the BAM lobby, I sighted Janice, still with her Veronica Lake long blond hair, standing alone by the information kiosk. Eagerly I approached her, and we greeted one another warmly. She was waiting for a friend, and so was I.

Janice asked me how I'd been.

"Fine," I said. "And you?"

"Good," she said, "good."

I took the plunge. "Are you still playing poker?" I asked.

"Oh yes," she said. "Still the same game."

"That's good," I said. I was emboldened to continue.

"You know, don't you," I said, reassured I could be calm but wanting her to learn the truth, "that I was kicked out of the poker game?" I felt like one of Dante's sinners who has only one precious moment to tell his story.

"No!" she said clearly shocked. "Really? You were kicked out?!"

"Yes. Leslie wrote me a letter."

"Why?" she asked, still visibly stunned.

"I don't know," I said. "Maybe the bike trip. I don't think she ever forgave me. And other stuff too. Who knows?"

"Wow!" she said.

"So no one said anything about it?" I asked. "How did they explain my absence?"

"Oh, I think Miriam just said you weren't coming. It seemed odd, but I thought maybe you'd grown tired of the game. Remember how we talked about how to keep it interesting."

"No," I said. "I loved the game. Really loved it." A lilt of nostalgia had crept into my voice. I shifted to a lower register.

"I'm playing in another game now, on Long Island," I told her matter-of-factly.

"Are you?" she said. "That's great!"

"Yes, another game. It's women again."

This was true. About two years earlier, I'd been phoned by an acquaintance on Long Island, where I had my new country house, and asked if I would like to play poker. This group also began the evening with snacks or a light dinner and then played cards. The level of play was somewhat higher than that of my old group, as were the stakes, but I managed to keep up and was asked back. Most, though not all, of the women who played were lesbians, so no one told penis jokes. Sometimes the gossip about who was breaking up with whom seemed a little stifling. But, all in all, I liked going. It was a much looser group than my old group, with no fixed schedule or membership. Sometimes I was called to play and sometimes I wasn't. I liked the lesser intensity.

Janice and I chatted a bit more. She was doing well, she said. And had I heard that Neil was dead?

"Yes," I said. "How terrible."

I spotted my friend coming into the building and knew I had only a minute more.

"Great to see you, Janice," I said, lingering for a moment as we hugged. I looked up into her face. "You know," I said, the resolve forming in me as I spoke, "you might tell them at poker that you ran in to me and that I'm in another game. In fact, tell them that I played with Bella Abzug. I played in her last poker game, the week before she died."

"Did you really?" she exclaimed. "I'll tell them. It was great to see you, Jenny."

6

Yes, I had played poker with Bella Abzug. I had even taught Bella how to play anaconda, the game in which you pass cards to the right or left and have to break up your original hand.

"That's not poker," barked Bella, sitting at the poker table in one of her great hats. The game was at her house in Noyac. It was odd to encounter Bella Abzug in a conventionally pleasant postmodern house in the Hamptons. Grumbling, she went along with anaconda and won the hand.

Bella's favorite game was three-card monte, a game of

nerve. You get one card up and two cards down. The bets are a dollar, two dollars, and three. With raises, there can be nine dollars riding on a single bet. The perfect high is two aces; the perfect low is ace, deuce. If your first card isn't very high or very low, the odds tell you to fold. Playing three-card monte with Bella, I learned to stay in, bet high, and even to win on a bluff. I played with Bella perhaps four or five times over the course of a year and a half. Then I heard she was very ill.

One of the regulars called to set up a game. Bella had been in and out of the hospital, but she was a little better and had come out to Noyac for a mild spring weekend. She wanted to play poker.

When I arrived at Bella's house in the twilight of that May evening and went inside, I encountered her as on other nights, seated with her hat on at the table set up for our game. She looked more worn but still seemed herself. An oxygen hookup was attached under her nose, which she removed when we started playing poker. "How are you, Bella?" we asked. "Eh," said Bella, and made a face. She told us she was all right sitting, but she found the slightest physical exertion exhausting.

That night Bella Abzug, who would die the next week, played poker from seven-thirty to midnight. We played several hands of three-card monte and all the other games we knew as well. At the end of the evening, when people said they were tired and wanted to quit, she gave them a hard time but perhaps with a little less force and fewer insults than usual. After she hooked up her oxygen, two people from the game, each holding one of her arms, helped her rise from the table and cross the room. That process took a long, long time.

I wasn't able to attend the first game held after Bella's death. The women who played all brought hats and wore them throughout the evening. I was sorry to miss the game, our poker memorial for Bella, but my friend who went said it didn't really work. One couldn't play poker and mourn Bella at the same time. In our recent games, we have always mentioned Bella's name when we've decided to play three-card monte. And maybe, because of Bella, we've played it more often. Otherwise, we think of her only a little. Or at least that's the case with me. The game, after all, commands your attention. In the final analysis, a given player is expendable. Perhaps that's not something to be sad about. Still, I'd be curious to know if anyone in my old game ever misses me.

FAMILY ALBUM

I turned to hunt for my name in the index when the book arrived in the mail. Mine, my brother's, and, of course, our mother's. I was curious, but only mildly. Unopened, the packet had seemed mysterious. The unfamiliar logo on the corner of the padded envelope had promised the unexpected—a novel, work of criticism, maybe an anthology—to read and add to my shelves. I like the ritual of opening mail. It always stirs in me a small excitement, which no amount of junk mail and bills, not even the occasional personal or professional rejection letter, can quite quell. In this case, though, as soon as I saw that the book inside the packet was the old man's memoir, my expectation shriveled. Oh that, I sighed. "So he actually finished." I noted the vanity press. "We invite the friends of Jake Salzman to share . . ."

Jake's had seemed one of those end-of-life projects: an

old screenwriter whose career had linked him with a few events and luminaries of his time, writing memoirs the world was in no way waiting for. When he had phoned me in New York to ask for photos, I had sent off two, but not without a moment's concern as to how I might retrieve them if he died. Such worry did seem a little mean-spirited. It's okay if they are lost, I told myself.

Still, when Jake had returned the pictures, accompanied by a jaunty note, I had wasted no time putting them back where they belonged. Finding the empty photo corners on a page in my childhood album, I had slipped back the snapshot of the three of us on Malibu Beach: me six that summer, with my hair cropped short, wearing my wrinkled shorts and T-shirt; my younger brother, Peter, also in rumpled shorts, making one of his funny faces into the camera; and Jake between us, spreading his arms to encompass us both, the trusted family friend. The second picture Jake returned, the studio publicity shot of our mother, went back into a separate envelope. Jean Harmon's career as a symbol of glamour remained for me distinct from our history as a family.

A brief entry in the index sent me flipping through the text. I knew that Peter and I were the most minor of supporting characters, serving only to lend a little color and context to the main interest of Jake's relationship with our mother. I had been surprised when I learned of the affair because I thought our mother had found him too unattractive. "Jake always liked me," she said, "but I couldn't be more involved with him because of his clammy hands." She had a way of cutting a suitor down to size, whether he was a current flame or a distant ember. Our small fatherless family drew together in the exuberance of her benign contempt for her lovers, and for men in general. Men, she said, are like children and need to be treated like children. Peter and I, her actual children, listened and absorbed such pronouncements. Once when she was talking about a housekeeper who had left to get married but then become clinically depressed during menopause, Peter was unable to contain himself. "Oh, there you go again, '*men* of course!'" he exclaimed. Peter's impassioned, unintentional pun became a favorite family story.

One of our mother's suitors had worn a ridiculous cummerbund, so she had not been able to marry him. One was a multimillionaire, but he wouldn't let Peter and me have dessert at a fancy restaurant, so that was it for the millionaire—some other woman snagged him. One had got his penis stuck in the zipper of his trousers and had to be rushed to the nearby hospital in Santa Monica—I remembered that particular drama, which had occurred at the beach the summer I was ten. One, but for his tiny feet might have been a great athlete, a deficiency that inspired our mother to think of writing a story called "Athlete's Foot." And Jake, someone we had respected, who played Ping-Pong with Peter and me in our backyard and talked straight, had those hands.

Jake and I had a particular bond. We were pegged as cerebral, the type who calmly, clearly think things through, unlike my smart but impetuous mother and my dreamy brother. When I grew up, Jake made a clumsy pass at me. It upset me, the shifting of categories, but I forgave him, and a few years later invited him to my wedding, to which he came wearing his new toupee. He flirted with my friends there, and I felt sad for him in his lifelong lack of physical beauty.

I learned about the affair right after my mother died.

"Where were we kids?" I asked as we sat together in a Manhattan coffee shop, the seventy-five-year-old writer, thankfully no longer trusting to the transformative powers of the toupee, and the middle-aged child. Maybe my mother had been hard up, I thought to myself, but I didn't share the thought with Jake. At the time of their affair, my mother would have been almost fifty; Jake was ten years her junior.

"Oh, you were asleep, I guess," Jake answered, with a laugh of recollected pleasure.

And at eighty, he had written about us all, boasting of his sexual conquest of the beautiful Jean Harmon and, reaching almost fifty years into the past, remembering me with that one disturbing sentence.

"I was touched by Jean's children," he had written. "Jenny, five or six, was slim, dark, shy, and perpetually troubled by some unvoiced anxiety."

As I read this, at fifty-five "nearly old," as my friends and I marveled to one another but hardly believed, a person with grown children and dead parents—the absent father and the scintillating mother both gone so that sometimes I would gasp at my own survival—the portrait of this worried child, who was me, jumped off the page as an exposure and indictment. It didn't help that the very next sentence described Peter—Petie, he was then—as "sunny, open, a blond angel of innocence." I had worked hard since childhood to be open, too. It almost felt like a betrayal that Jake should cut back to that core of fear in me. That night I sat at a dinner party, with muscles taut between my eyes and mouth. The old anxiety buzzed and clattered within, so that I could hardly hear the banter around me. I felt the people at the table must be able to see it.

2

At the ocean I had always felt safe and calm. Our mother would send us off to Malibu every summer from June to September and then herself commute from town to be with us as much as she could. I knew all the creatures and signs of creatures of the sand and sea—the gulls flying overhead, dropping their stray feathers on the beach, which became excellent pens for writing in the sand, the sea anemones in shallow pools, the mussels clinging to the rocks, the shells, the seaweed. I would lie on the warm white sand, digging with one hand down to the cool dampness beneath, digging the deepest holes in which to bury Petie. We ran into the surf, laughing to catch the waves and ride them in on our rubber rafts. At night I nestled in my bed, soothed by the breaking of the surf on one side of the house and the large trucks rumbling past on the Pacific Coast Highway on the other.

The housekeeper took care of us, but our mother would return most evenings, standing out front of the beach house with the surf lapping about her ankles to catch the last rays of the setting sun. She loved to inhale the sea air in sensuous, dramatic breaths. I wasn't anxious then, though sometimes when we all were in the car, driving on the winding road between the beach and the house in town, I worried when I couldn't see the road ahead of us. If I couldn't see it, it must not be there. Our car would surely tumble into the void.

I wouldn't have called myself anxious. *Anxiety* is not a word children use. I was wary—of strangers, of new foods, of intrusions in general. And I was careful—to do well in school, to keep my things together, to keep Petie out of my room when I was counting the pennies from my piggy bank and putting them in neat little piles organized by year— shiny recently minted coins of the early fifties, duller piles representing the forties, a single coin here and there of the thirties or even twenties. When the task was done, I would call out that Petie could come in again, and he'd come trotting in, blond and eager and seemingly forgiving. We played together all the time, pretending to be cowboys or imagining ourselves the chief counselors of a sleep-away camp called the Happy Club. Its members were an eclectic mix of humans, ducks, and seals, whom Petie and I would pretend to discipline when they transgressed in raiding the camp candy store. Petie joined me in having this authority, but I made sure to keep the upper hand over my younger brother. I could always beat Petie at Ping-Pong, an order of things that to me seemed natural but later it turned out he had resented. He had raged to me about it quite recently, though our childhood was almost forty years in the past. I was glad he seemed not to remember my strategy, if ever he got ahead in the game, to remind him that he wet his bed. Invariably he would then get upset and lose.

"All those years," he said, "that you beat me at Ping-Pong. Do you remember?"

"Yes," I replied, thinking how mean it had been to call him Stinky. I had bought a Ping-Pong table for the basement of my new country house on Long Island. Peter had visited and, despite my fiercest effort to maintain my old supremacy, had beaten me decisively.

"Well, I realized when I came to your house and beat you—and you hated my beating you, don't deny it—that the only reason you won all those years was because you were older!" He spoke with intensity, giving a thump to the table of the diner where we were eating and quarreling to punctuate the word *older*.

"That makes sense," I said. "But you're wrong about me needing to win. I try hard, that's all." I wondered if I was telling the truth. On balance, I thought I was, especially as I looked at the angry, somewhat dissipated face across the table from me. But for the pain his expressions conveyed, I felt almost like laughing. It seemed foolish that a middle-aged man, grayer than I was, though three and a half years younger, should be so worked up about a history of Ping-Pong. It wasn't really Ping-Pong, though, that by then was the trouble between us.

3

I never blamed Peter for what had occurred when we were so young. He wasn't yet twenty and I was twenty-two. When it was over—and how incredible that the whole business should last only fifteen minutes—the one certainty in my mind was that we could never tell our mother. That seemed ironic, since surely but for her it would never have happened. Our mother's body, which we had cuddled on weekend mornings in her big king-sized bed and been dazzled by as she slipped it into her sequined evening gowns, had been the magnet that kept us fixed within our home and family. I could not imagine growing up and leaving, though unlike Peter, I always excelled at school, at least in terms of all those straight-A report cards. It hadn't been easy to venture out from the shelter of my home. The first day of kindergarten had been a great trial. My mother had dutifully remained for the first half-hour to nod encouragement from the side of the room, but then she had left me to cope without her. The teacher had organized a game of musical chairs, in which I could remember sidling in terror from one small wooden chair to another, listening, as if for eternal silence, for the music to stop. What if I were not in front of a chair when the music stopped? What if I were eliminated from the game? The prospect seemed my annihilation.

But fear and desolation had never stopped me. You might say that was my strength, how always, I persisted. My kindergarten teacher had told my mother I would go far, a prediction my mother often repeated to me as part of our nightly bedtime chat. The bracing "you will go far," would be coupled with the more palliative "your time will come" when I confessed to my lack of popularity at school. I never quite believed her, but hadn't she been right? With its mix of mistakes and fulfillment, my life would have to be called basically successful. I sometimes wondered what our mother had said at bedtime to Peter. *His* teachers, from kindergarten on, were always talking about his potential. Our mother was eager to divide the goods of life fairly—"even Stevens," she insisted. So Peter got endowed with sexiness and imagination to offset the fact that I was acknowledged to be better at everything else from school to sports to being a responsible person.

So it was Petie, although he was three years younger, who was ahead of me in sexual experience. I remember him coming home from a party at which the children had played spin the bottle. "I did it, I did it," he exulted. I at that point had had one mortifying "date," arranged largely by my mother. The boy, Tommy, who had been somehow persuaded to escort me to the semiformal school dance, turned up at our house in his T-shirt and sneakers. As soon as we arrived at the dance hall, he bolted to a corner to skulk there for the evening with a group of boys. I couldn't decide if I was more humiliated or relieved to be rid of him.

When Petie was twelve and I fifteen, he offered to give me kissing lessons. My memory is hazy, but I half-remember one brief lesson, aborted in mutual disgust. There is no doubt, though, that I said yes on an afternoon seven years later. Just out of college, a Seven Sisters graduate now working for a pittance in a New York publishing house, I was staying at our mother's East Sixties luxury apartment. Peter had come to see me from his tenement on the Lower East Side, where he was living with his girlfriend and his dog, after dropping out of college for the second time. He was trying to be a film-maker. It was a dreary day in March, and we were bored.

"What shall we do?" I asked.

"I know what we can do," said Peter, lounging in an over-sized blue silk armchair and raising the eyebrows on his handsome face.

Sitting opposite him on the matching sofa, I couldn't say how I knew his meaning, but I did. "No," I said, firmly shaking my head for good measure.

"Why not?" asked Peter.

"I don't know why not," I said. I looked at him in disbelief. It was a game. Truth or Dare.

So we had gone into my room and taken off our clothes.

When he turned away from me, I noticed a discoloration along his spine, and that surprised me. I went into the bathroom and put in my diaphragm. My mother had made sure I got fitted with one when I graduated from college. By now it had seen a little but not a lot of use. "All right," I said, stepping back into the room.

Thinking afterward about the experience, what struck me most forcibly was the lack of any tenderness. Petie kept his head averted and finished quickly. To the few friends in whom I confided, I marveled, "He went at me as if I were a whore." I had felt numb, totally numb throughout the brief ordeal.

"You okay?" Petie asked that afternoon, as he left to go back home.

"Sure," I said. "And you?"

"Oh yeah," Petie said.

Later that evening, I stood barefoot in my nightgown on the terrace of the apartment, letting the rain soak me through and through. I developed a terrible cold, took antibiotics for ten days, and somehow felt purged of my brother, as if I'd had a bloodletting.

I knew at once that our experiment had been a mistake. It had been a mistake because it wasn't fun and because it had hurt my feelings. I wondered if it might have been nicer if it had been tender. But how could tenderness have been possible? How would we then have got on with our separate lives?

For many years I would have said that what had happened had meant nothing and that it changed nothing. Peter and I were as we had always been, a brother and sister who because of geography—he went back out West; I stayed in the East—had increasingly little contact but who kept in touch and always felt connected. On two occasions he again proposed having sex. Once was just a few years after the initial incident, and I said to him, "You must be crazy." The second time was when our mother was dying. We went together to her apartment, which happened to be near the hospital, and had both lain down to rest on the only bed. I was forty-five, Peter forty-two. I felt him sidling up to me. "Peter!" I said. "What are you doing?"

"I guess I'm horny," Peter said, with a half-apologetic chuckle

"Don't," I said and proceeded to take my nap.

Later I had a different awareness. Decades after what had happened between me and my brother, when incest survivors started telling their stories, I understood what they meant when they spoke of feeling annihilated.

4

"You were older," said Peter in the same diner argument that touched on the Ping-Pong. I was beginning to see what my being three years older had meant to him. "You should have stopped it. Why didn't you?"

I had already been challenged with Peter's question by my daughter, Sarah—or almost his question—when I had felt compelled to tell her about my brother and me. "Why did you do it?" Sarah asked.

5

Earlier that summer, lying on the beach in East Hampton, the beach near my new house with the Ping-Pong table in the basement, I had a premonition. As I did most late afternoons, I had ridden my bike to the ocean, spread my towel on the sand, and stretched out, with my straw hat drawn over my head, to daydream and doze. I felt deeply the old peace that the ocean and the sand had always given me. All my worries magically receded.

Today, though, a sudden thought caused me to raise my head from the towel and swing into a cross-legged position.

"I bet he'll try something," I thought— I almost *knew* it. "I know him," I said out loud to the waves.

Sarah, my adventurous daughter, had been traveling out West, hopping from one friend to another, sometimes hitchhiking, which seemed to me so dangerous. "I can handle it," Sarah said in one of her infrequent phone conversations with me.

"You need to rethink that," I said, despairing. I was relieved to learn Sarah would be stopping in California to see Peter—Peter and his nice second wife, Erica, to whom he had been married for seventeen years. With my own failed marriage behind me, I admired, even envied, his largely settled domesticity.

"Try to talk her out of hitchhiking," I said to my brother over the phone. I liked it when we cooperated in dealing with our children. In a way it brought back our partnership in "the Happy Club."

"I'll try," Peter promised. "But she *is* grown up, you know."

"Well, why doesn't she act grown up?" I replied.

Lying on the beach that day, the thought disturbing my routine and reverie was that Peter could not be trusted with my daughter. I felt like rushing to call him, to say whatever would restrain him. "You might be tempted . . ." "Do not . . ." "Do not dare to . . ." "I forbid . . ." But then the intervention seemed tricky. It might insult him. It might even *give* him the idea. Also Sarah could be pretty tough. If she could fend off truck drivers, couldn't she handle Peter? Fearful and uncertain, I decided to wait. I vowed, though, as I stood up and inhaled my last deep breath of sea air before turning to head home, that if he made the slightest advance, I would tell Sarah my own story. What this would accomplish I couldn't quite say. At the least it would provide a context. Sarah would know she was not to blame. She would see the family picture.

<h1 style="text-align:center">6</h1>

I talked briefly with Sarah when she arrived at her uncle's house. "Enjoy yourself with Peter and Erica," was all I said. "And don't do any more hitchhiking!"

"We'll see," Sarah said.

Then a few days after Sarah had left him, I got a call from my brother. He reported having put Sarah on a bus to her next destination, and for that I thanked him. I sensed, though, that something was wrong. Peter sounded edgy, as he did again in a second call a week later. And it was unusual for him to be phoning so often.

"Any word from Sarah?" he asked, sounding anxious.

"No," I said. "But I'll be seeing her. She's coming here at the end of the summer. That is, if she survives the hitchhiking!"

Telling Peter I'd be seeing Sarah soon was my way of saying, "I don't yet know what you've done, but whatever it is, you're not going to get away with it. For now, let's still pretend it's only Sarah we're concerned about."

At last, triumphant from her adventures on the road and her thwarting of predictions of disaster, Sarah arrived on Long Island. Spirited, messy, always surprising, she blew like a gusty wind through my quiet house. In part to diffuse her energy, I suggested we go to the beach. "Let's walk," Sarah said, when we had spread out our towels on the sand. We strode along at a pace slightly too fast for me with the surf lapping over our feet. Suddenly, Sarah, slowing, took hold of my arm. "I've got something to tell you," she said. "Will you promise to keep it secret?"

I felt an anticipatory rush of agitation and knowledge. Turning toward her, I steadied myself to be attentive. "If I can," I said. I looked at Sarah and waited.

"I want to tell you about Uncle Peter," Sarah said, "but I don't want what I say to get back to him."

I took a sharp little breath, mustering my forces. "Let *me* deal with that," I said. "Tell me your story."

What Sarah told me in the next half-hour corresponded in the main to what I heard later from Peter. Sarah left out that she had carved her own and her uncle's initials on a tree. Peter left out that when he had found Sarah sunbathing naked at his house, he had taken off his own clothes to show her nudity was not something to be embarrassed about. Otherwise the two accounts tallied. I didn't need Peter's account to believe Sarah's, but when I had heard both, it soothed me a little that they were the same, that Sarah hadn't exaggerated and Peter hadn't minimized what happened.

The key events had all transpired while Peter's wife, Erica, was off at work. On day one of the visit, thinking her uncle would be out for a while longer, Sarah had removed her clothes to bask in the California sun of Peter's geranium-and cactus-filled garden. When her uncle unexpectedly returned, she had scurried in embarrassment to dress herself, and he had then *un*dressed.

On day two they had gone for a walk together, and Sarah had agreed when Peter suggested there had always been sexual vibes between them. Maybe so, I reflected. I remembered Sarah as a little girl rumpling Peter's tousled hair. "Oh, Uncle Peter, you have such wild hair!" My seven-year-old daughter's abandon had startled me. I had been awed by its boldness.

On day three they had taken another walk, and Peter had said to Sarah, "I guess you need an uncle more than another lover."

On day four, allowing herself a delayed reaction to his impropriety, Sarah had excoriated Peter as he drove her to the bus station.

"But she really let me have it," Peter said, when finally I called him. "I think your daughter is a very angry person."

In a sense not much had happened. But I knew that if Sarah had been receptive, Peter would have had sex with my daughter. What was unforgivable was not so much what had happened but what might have.

As I had planned to do, I told Sarah about Peter and me, right there and then as we were walking in the afternoon sunlight on the beach. Raising the subject embarrassed me, but I tried to be matter-of-fact. I also tried to be fair to Peter, emphasizing that I had gone along with his proposal. "Why?" asked Sarah, who seemed more intrigued than shocked.

"I don't know," I said. "I didn't really feel I had a choice."

"Well, I'm not you," Sarah said.

"No, thank God you're not," I said. In that moment I believed in progress.

7

I waited to telephone Peter until I was calmer. I was frightened by the pitch and pressure of my anger, and I didn't want to lose my only brother. One day, without planning to, I simply picked up the phone.

Peter readily admitted to what had happened and said he had been expecting my call.

"But Peter," I said, "what you did was terrible. You tried to seduce my daughter!"

"I know, I know," Peter said, with his slight stammer. I listened hard. I wondered if he did know.

"What were you thinking?" I asked.

"I can't tell you," Peter said. "You know, I love Erica, but she's fifty now and has a fifty-year-old body. I keep being attracted to young women."

I didn't say, "What about *your* fifty-year-old body?" but I thought it and felt a wave of blistering contempt for him. Peter would have said it was the contempt for men I had learned from our mother.

Later I thought about my own aging body. But not during the phone call.

"Mom didn't teach us morals," offered Peter, lamely.

"Bullshit," I said. The understanding surged in me of our mother, who may have dallied with people and even used them but who didn't fool herself.

"Anyway," I said, "you could have learned them on your own."

"Sarah was provocative," Peter said. "She was sunbathing naked."

"Peter," I said. My brother seemed to me like a slippery

calf, and I was the cowhand trying to corral him. Every time I thought I had him cornered, he wriggled out again. I flung out my moral lasso one more time.

"Peter, you're her uncle. If she were masturbating in your bed, you're her uncle. It's your role and duty to protect her."

Later I was proud of myself for the wit and bite of that last remark. As soon as I got off the phone, I assessed it as my best shot. I was glad, too, that for the first time since it happened, we had talked about our own sexual encounter. I told Peter that it had been harmful to me but that I didn't blame him. In part, this was to make the point that I *did* blame him in his conduct with Sarah. "You betrayed me and you betrayed Sarah," I told him, just like that, a straightforward statement made without rancor. I felt calm. It was calm stemming from concentration and not from self-restraint. Peter wasn't calm at all. Throughout the conversation he hemmed and hawed, alternating between apologies and self-defense.

I said what I wanted to say, I assessed after hanging up. And I hadn't worried about consequences—that felt liberating as well. I hadn't lost my temper, but I hadn't equivocated either.

8

About six months later, Peter and I met and quarreled in the diner. He almost stormed out, but I asked him to sit down and keep talking to me. "I guess you're still my sister,"

Peter said as we parted at the subway, but he sounded as if he wasn't sure. Shortly, he went off to make a documentary in China, where he and Erica stayed for over a year. He didn't send me his usual Christmas card, and I felt anxious that I hadn't heard from him. I had decided I wanted us to move on from what had happened. When I knew he was back in California, I phoned him. On hearing mine, his voice sounded strained.

"I'm not sure I was ready to talk to you," Peter said. "Or am even now. I've been thinking a lot about things, and I realize I'm very mad at you."

"Oh, " I said, taken aback. "I guess I was mad at you too."

"About what?" asked Peter.

"You know, what happened with Sarah," I said, reluctant to broach this again.

"Oh that," Peter said. "You know, for a long time I thought I was just a shit. But then I woke up. I decided I'm just not going to feel bad about that anymore. Sarah's a very troubled young woman."

My instinct was to be careful. "What are *you* mad about?" I asked. My brother seemed sadly beyond my reach.

A list followed of grievances, some dating back to our childhood. It was detailed.

"And in 1985," Peter said, "you snubbed me."

"Remind me what happened," I said. "I'm afraid I don't remember."

"You silenced me," Peter said. "And at my own party." Peter elaborated how at a party in his honor, an event organized to celebrate one of his documentaries, he had been talking to someone quite important. I had come up and said, "We don't need to go into that." Remembering this made him furious.

I listened to Peter's case against me, and then felt I couldn't hear any more of this.

"You know," I said, "probably we both have reasons to be angry. But what do you want to do? We can stay alienated. That's an option. And one day one of us will hear the other is dead."

"No, no, I don't want that," Peter replied, alarmed. I remembered he had always been a softie.

"But I don't want to deal with someone who has such a negative sense of me," I said. I felt bold in what I was saying. "I'm sick of being the nasty, stodgy, older sister. That's not me. I need to feel that you like me."

Peter said he would think about it.

When I hung up, I tried to remember the incident in 1985. Yes, I had come up to him at the party and found him talking to a stranger about our mother's sex life, telling a risqué story about one of her lovers. I couldn't bear my brother being glib about our mother, heedless of her dignity and reputation. That's when I had said, "We don't need to go into that." In my mind, I wasn't snubbing Peter, although now I understood I had embarrassed him. I was doing what I had always done, what I was doing still, defending our home and family.

That had been my task—for all my life. Was it any wonder I had always been anxious? Thinking about my effort, my relentless vigilance—and what had it come to?—I felt worn out. As a child I had glared at the men I didn't like and believed I could make them go away. I was the gatekeeper, the one saying who should be admitted into our inner sanctum and who expelled from it. Such was my self-appointed role, and I took it on with a passion that sometimes impelled my mother to contemplate me and declare herself positively afraid of her fierce little daughter. And always, I had chosen not to know when sex was going on in the house.

Looking back, I saw my resolve and I saw my sacrifice. I had been so busy keeping sex at bay as it might touch my mother that my own sexual flowering had been tentative and restrained. Later I had done my best to catch up, managing even with some panache, but never without an undercurrent of dread, never with Peter's open, dramatic, persuasive sensuality. I had had to go to bed with him. That way I could hope to get back some relinquished part of myself. Only it hadn't worked.

Alone in my New York apartment, I turned to my bookshelf. I scanned it for Jake Salzman's memoir, which recently I had stashed unread on a shelf of books written by family friends. I took the book in my hand and looked up the references to Jean Harmon.

"A tall leggy blonde." "Delicately assembled, nicely rounded." "A stunner even in the land of starlets."

Men, I thought. Jake was describing Jean when he first had met her—and I reckoned she had truly been put off by his clammy hands. He could look but not touch, I reflected. The thought gave me some satisfaction.

Then it was years later, the early fifties. Jake reencountered a woman who was aging.

"But she had faded slightly. Although she still tossed off an occasional high kick, faint bulges marred the former chorus girl's calves that had once captivated Ziegfeld."

What a disgusting little prick he is, I thought. I was indignant for my mother.

With seduction, the cocky flesh-appraiser turned psychologically penetrating man of feeling. I read his account: "Jean saw sex as a smashing of taboos, a wicked indulgence enhanced by naughty language. It seemed for her a private release, devoid of emotion, rather than the tender blending I sought. The act appeared more important to Jean than the person she shared it with. She liked to schedule sexual encounters almost like a tennis match, and sometimes with less warm up."

I closed the book and put it away. I didn't like what Jake had written, but I believed it. So that's what she was like, I thought, at least with him.

Jake's description of my mother made me think as well about Peter. *A private release.* No *time for warm up.* So many siblings grow up to have nothing in common, as one goes into business and the other becomes an artist, one turns born-again Christian while the other stays a liberal Democrat. That didn't apply with Peter and me. We had the same politics, read the same books, found the same things odd and funny, and, of course, shared our own peculiar history. No one else in the world knew what it had been like to grow up in that family. Here was a bond so compelling that many mornings I woke up thinking I couldn't bear losing it and him. Yet in the incident with Sarah, something irrevocable had happened. I didn't want that to be the case, but it was. To accept the change, without willfulness or rancor, brought me a sad kind of peace. Maybe Peter really didn't have morals, at least not sexual ones. I couldn't say, because I realized that I didn't understand his way of being sexual in the world. In truth, I hardly understood my own but sensed it was different. If not more moral, then more personal. We had started off together, giggling and roughhousing under the covers when our mother let us into her bed. Her body and her use of it had bound and mesmerized us both. But where had we gone from there? If we had understood our different paths better, we might have been less disappointed in one another. We might have had fewer misunderstandings.

Some months later, as a way of not altogether losing touch, I sent Peter a photo of Sarah holding her eight-month-old baby boy, a child whom the dauntless Sarah had had with a New Orleans trumpeter. The trumpeter had departed, and now Sarah was raising the child on her own. The picture was lovely, and though I retained no duplicate, I wanted Peter to have it. Taking after our side of the family, Sarah's son reminded me of Peter—I thought he looked a lot like Peter had as a baby, especially in the shape of the eyes and nose and in the open trusting expression. I couldn't figure out if I was saying to Peter, "Look how Sarah has survived, and it's not you she's holding." Or if I was saying, "It *is* you. This reminds me of you. Please come to your senses."

Peter did not write back. Our mother, I thought, would have been heartbroken. She had wanted us to stick together.

HER HAIR

I remember my mother lamenting the change in her hair. She was eighty-one, three years away from dying, though that was not my worry then, and perhaps not even hers. She put the tips of her fingers to her tousled gray curls. "I used to have such lovely thick hair," she said. "You can't imagine how lovely and thick it was.

"But your hair is lovely now," I said. "And I don't see that it's not thick."

I meant what I said. I liked how she looked as an old lady, the way she had grown lighter in body and spirit. Especially I liked her hair. Short, unstudied, just a touch unruly, it added to the gamine look that seemed new and that quite charmed me. Whether to hide her hair or, as a purely practical matter, to keep her head warm, or both, she almost always wore a hat—a little navy blue straw hat with an upturned brim. The hat, the cane, the image of her as she hobbled along in her Reeboks, the only shoes, she said, that accommodated her bunion—these are things I remember.

Certainly I liked her hair better than all those years in which she had dyed it blond—then it could look like straw. And thank God she no longer wore that terrible blond wig, reminding me of an artichoke, that she had insisted on donning for social occasions throughout her sixties, even into her seventies. I found the wig in her closet when she died, stashed on the shelf above the bag of diapers. I'm sure they're not called diapers. Some euphemism surely has been devised to mask their sad necessity.

Now, though, it's my hair that's the problem. I noticed the other day that I can see through it. My hair had seemed peculiar and hard to get looking right for some time, but I had thought this just the drying-out effect of winter. Then suddenly, seeing right through it, especially on top in the front, I understood that I had suffered what my friend Hannah calls a *coup de vieux*, one of those dramatic capitulations to aging from which there is no rebounding or reversal. I stood there peering through my hair, as if continuing to look at it might make it sprout again. Of course, I only saw through it all the more clearly, no matter what I tried to imagine and believe. Not that its sorry thinness is something that leaps out at you. To others, I probably just look a little older, a little more worn down. They might not quite know

why. But I do. My awareness made me shudder at my image
in the mirror.

I used to wish for fine straight hair, so I could grow it long
down my back and flip it casually with my hand or a toss of
my head. The hair I was endowed with—dark brown in contrast to my mother's natural honey blond—was thick, sometimes unmanageably thick, and somewhere between wavy
and curly. In my forties, I cut it short and chic and went gray
more gracefully, so my friends said, than many other
women. I'd have ranked my hair right behind my eyes and
my bosom in my list of good features. I wasn't a great beauty as my mother had been. From something she once said to
me, I realized that she had had an absolute confidence in her
beauty every time she walked into a room. This is what came
into my mind when she lamented the thinning of her hair—
her beauty and her knowledge of it, the self-assurance it had
given her in facing the world. My mother had always told me
it was inner beauty that counted—something, I've noticed,
that very beautiful people often say. I don't mean to imply a
note of insincerity, but I think outer beauty counts for them
too. I felt for my mother mourning her lost golden hair; yet
the quality of this loss seemed something I would never
share. In a strange way, this seemed to offer me a chance of
greater contentment.

My own looks had always been perfectly fine, at least not
something to worry about. Perhaps my vanity lay in that—

in knowing I didn't have to worry, knowing I passed muster, that I was pretty enough and to some even enticing. When I was forty-four and single again after seventeen years of marriage, a young man asked me to go away with him for the weekend.

"Why would you want to do that?" I laughed.

"So I could profit from your wisdom and beauty," he replied, hurt, I surmised, that I should laugh at him. Now ten years later, it turns out he's living on my street. I felt ashamed when, recently, dashing out in old clothes from my building to buy the newspaper, I ran directly into him, almost colliding, before recovering enough to stammer his name. *He* looked all right, maybe fifteen pounds heavier and with a little less hair, but I felt as though I'd turned into his grandmother. I tried to tell myself I was only fifty-five and still only nineteen years older than he is. But I knew that everything had changed. In our earlier encounter I had been bolstered by a pleasant sense of myself as "*une femme d'un certain âge.*" Now, though, I couldn't imagine that a younger man might still desire me. Hadn't I joined the near old? On a recent date with a man who is my contemporary, we had talked about our grown children, our aches and pains, and our pension plans.

I think it's a sign of my weakened self-confidence that I've started sneaking into movies as a senior citizen. A friend told me she had done this, and I was sure I looked as old as

she. Usually there's a young person selling the tickets, and
how does someone young tell the difference between fifty-
five and sixty-two, especially when I push my glasses down
my nose, squint, and add a little quaver to my voice in making my request? "One senior for . . ." I've gotten in this way
now maybe ten or twelve times. No one has questioned me,
though it's poignant that I still expect to be challenged, or
you might say it's more poignant that I feel the need to *feign*
decrepitude in order to have the scam succeed. Facing the
second hurdle of the person collecting tickets at the door, I
try to hunch over and maintain my squint as I hand over the
ticket. My heart pounds as I glance into the ticket collector's
face, afraid, yet half-hoping, to detect in it signs of disbelief.
Sometimes, too, back when I'm purchasing the ticket, I act
befuddled about the time of the movie I want to see and
even its title. Sometimes I *am* befuddled. And decrepit.
Often now, coming home from work, I walk heavily up the
steps from the subway platform, my knees stiff and uncertain, while young men bound by me three steps at a time.

I used to bound. As a child, I climbed over the breakwa-
ter rocks at the beach like an exuberant antelope. As a
woman, into my thirties and forties, I still felt like Hermes,
a fleet-footed tomboy. I called myself an athlete, even when,
increasingly, what that came to mean was its price in aches
and pains—my knees, my feet, my elbow, my lower back.
Even now, I can manage to get beyond these. And again I

move into the zone in which my body extends almost to match my imagination.

But I don't still feel like a tomboy, even in those transcendent moments. The tomboy pulled up stakes along with the temptress. Both stole away a year or so ago when I wasn't paying attention.

I sometimes think I am lucky that I wasn't older when my mother died, that I wasn't the age I am now.

"I feel so old," said my friend Hannah, who is fifty-eight. Hannah's ninety-two-year-old mother, Rose, is now in a nursing home, and Hannah visits her every day.

"It's not you who are old," I told her. "It's your mother."

"Isn't it the same thing?" she answered plaintively.

Before Rose went into the home, when her crisis of health and confidence was first upon her, she stayed for a month with her daughter and son-in-law, and, of course, she drove them both mad. I went over to help Hannah entertain her and to pay my respects.

A small, coiled figure with gnarled hands gripping the sides of an armchair that seemed too big for her, Rose didn't so much sit in as emanate from a corner of a room. "I used to wish my daughter long life," she confided to me in her accented English. "But noow"—she drew out the word—"I'm not so sure." She peered into the middle distance, intense, an ancient sibyl. "I was all right until I was ninety. And then . . . and then *something happened.*"

What does one say in response? "You'll be fine." Isn't that

a lie? Or, "I'm sorry." Do you offer condolences to someone for growing old? I think I said, "That sounds hard."

Rose nearly died after that—they said she couldn't last a week—but she rallied in the nursing home and is going amazingly strong. She's a spirited, relentless old lady, subtle in the battle with her daughter. Or is this only a daughter's perspective? Hannah feels her own life is over.

My mother, born two years before Rose, would be ninety-four now if she were still alive. A holy terror, I'm sure. She hated to be at a disadvantage. When she had her heart attack, she railed against the nurses in the hospital, accusing them of trying to kill her. I went to visit her right after the attack. Her hair was limp and lusterless. I remember thinking she looked like a dying cat whose fur has lost its gloss.

"I think I could eat some smoked salmon," she said to me, prone in her hospital bed, in an only slightly stagy whisper. "I would love it if you could you go up to Fraser Morris on Madison Avenue and buy me some of their delicious smoked salmon."

It was very hot out and I was rushed, needing to get back to my own house and children. When right up the street I saw Gristedes, there only one block from the hospital, I reasoned that their smoked salmon would surely do. My mother spat it out and called it salty. "Is this really Fraser Morris smoked salmon?" she asked. In truth, she could eat nothing. Her heart was half-destroyed. In the months before her death she grew as light as a sparrow.

Children see you as spoiled or imperious, and you're really only trying to get a little comfort. I've come to understand that. I also understand that it's hard to be relegated to the corner, to be expected to sit like Rose in the armchair, with all the ravages of age upon you, and graciously keep in your place. It's a place our culture has so ill defined. I'm sure Rose felt peripheral, yet for Hannah she took up all the space.

Last month I went to Paris to see my son, who married young and has two little girls. He and his wife have many friends who visit over bottles of wine, laughing and telling funny stories. My daughter-in-law was telling about her orthodontistry—a wry inconsequential tale. When she was young, her mother had accused her of sticking out her chin on purpose, but the problem was really her protruding bottom teeth. Then there were years of braces. And still she has a big chin.

As people laughed in response, teasing her about her chin, I thought of telling the story of *my* bottom teeth—of how I had worn braces for years and then my wisdom teeth undid the work, pushing my two front bottom teeth out of place. They had remained crooked, all my life. "See," I would have said, opening my mouth. "See how crooked they are."

I didn't say any of this. To do so seemed intrusive. But more than that, it seemed to me that my teeth didn't really count anymore. Why would anyone be interested in what I had done to fix them as a girl, when all they could be expected to do now was to fall out?

My mother would have shown her teeth, but I would have gritted mine while she was doing so, whether I was twenty or forty-five.

She died when I was forty-six, and that released me. In the eighteen months or so leading up to her death, I had felt, not old like Hannah, but in some profound way without a future. It had seemed wrong to be thriving when she was failing. It had seemed impossible that my life could continue after hers ended.

I say this. Yet it is equally true that I always resisted her, wary that if I didn't hold her off, she might consume me. So I wasn't one of those daughters who took infinite tender care of her old mother. I tell myself that she really didn't want me to. She was a woman who always took care of herself, right to the end, when she went down to Florida, hired round-the-clock nurses, and declared herself ready for death. But I didn't get the Fraser Morris smoked salmon. I would like to have done that. I would like to have done more.

She died; I missed her terribly. And I was free—in ways I had not been when she was alive. Exuberantly free of her scrutiny, I wrote a book, I had adventures. At fifty I boasted that aging couldn't dent me; I had just begun to have a fuller life. And then, and then, as Rose said, "something happened."

Now I feel I'm on the other side of some great divide, where much of the time I live among echoes and shadows.

I am death-brushed, a bit bewildered, and, above all, haunted by my mother. If I and this ghostly intimate were still at odds, this might be terrible. But we're not. I don't altogether know why, but the relationship has softened. My resentment of her, so strong in her life, has lifted like a blanket of fog that startlingly clears away. I can vaguely remember all those stories I used to relish and recount about her selfishness, her unmotherliness; but they seem distant and petty, no longer worth the indignant telling. My mother has become like an old friend whose follies are known but with whom it's pointless to be exasperated. That is not what's interesting. She also seems in some ways less like a mother than an older sibling, someone, as she returns to me at one age or another, who is almost my age. Or rather, she can never be older than eighty-four, and I keep creeping up on her. It no longer seems contradictory that she adored her grandchildren but also found them tiring. I can fathom how she cared what her children did, what opportunities they had and mistakes they made, and how that caring also had a limit, as she resisted feeling responsible for their lives. I understand how she could console herself for aging with material comfort and order in her life; for to my surprise, the otherworldliness I speak of notwithstanding, I perceive how I too can find pleasure in a neater house in which all the cooking utensils and stray magazines are in place, in little and not so little purchases from Bloomingdale's, in vacations where the thrill and even danger of distant places are buffered by luxury accommodations.

And I understand that vanity, and even desire, can survive in an aging body.

I have run into my young neighbor Jeff several times. After the first couple of encounters, I began to think twice before dashing out of the house in rags. Once I saw him when I was on my way to the theater, and I knew I looked good. That gave me satisfaction. We have talked about getting together for a walk or a drink.

I try to deflect my residue of lust—or is it just vanity?—by thinking of him as a candidate for my daughter, who is on her own with a young child. It both satisfies and causes me chagrin to think of handing him on to her—not, of course, that this is a transaction occurring in anyone's head but mine. He seems very nice, and I trust would be good to her. A strong part of the fantasy is also that he would be good to me, that as my son-in-law, his devotion to me, right down to the end of my life—and not just as his wife's mother but as a woman he once found attractive and always liked—would be steady and heartfelt. I am confident he would even come to the nursing home. His visits would be very cheering.

But I can only think of being in a nursing home, in this way, lightly, as a joke. Recently I consulted with a financial planner to get a better sense of my resources. "If you go into a nursing home at seventy-eight," she said, "do you agree that your discretionary expenses would decline by eighty percent?"

"Excuse me," I said. "Why are you putting me in a nursing home?"

"It's a standard part of the exercise," she said.

"At least make it eighty," I said, my life seeming over, my heart full of dread.

My mother never went into a nursing home. She kept her wits. Her insurance covered her home care. She died quickly.

At my thirty-fifth college reunion (which it seems important to note was held in a cluster with the two classes above us, so it was really only our thirty-*fourth*), the women in my class talked more than anything else about their mothers. Nine years earlier, at our far better attended and more buoyant twenty-fifth reunion, the talk had been of career aspirations, fulfilled and thwarted, of children going to good colleges or resisting this route, of marriages, divorces, and remarriages.

Now, sitting in a circle, peering into one another's faces and drawn to tell some central truth, mesmerized by the double vision of our twenty- and our fifty-five-year-old selves, we forty women talked about our mothers. Alive, dead, dying, remembered, our mothers still had us in their grip.

Some were shocking ghosts. "I never told anyone then," said Mary Watkins, "but my mother committed suicide when I was a freshman here."

Another woman had been raised by her younger aunts.

Her mother was in and out of psychiatric institutions. There she sat, fifty-five, with thinning gray hair and a beautiful, gaunt face—I remembered a plumpish rather homely dark-haired girl, whom I hadn't known well—speaking with intensity of how her younger aunts had really been her mothers, how she had come to see this only quite recently.

Other mothers were failing now and doing it peacefully or badly. Their daughters were finding new channels of love for them, or they were wearily, or warily—I had been one of the wary—doing whatever blood and complex feelings defined as necessary.

I took the plunge and introduced my particular ghost. "I'm better friends with my mother since she died," I said. "She used to be very difficult. But she's now she's so much more reasonable."

The group laughed. Someone agreed that this could happen. Still, the mood was somber. There we were, at fifty-five, all dwelling in the shadow of our mothers, which was a shadow touching and tingeing the future as well as the past. Sitting in that circle, talking about our mothers, we dramatized our own aging.

Later in the dorm lounge, nestled in the window seat where as an undergraduate I used to read while a woman two classes above me played Rodgers and Hart on the piano, I was nagged by the sense of something false. I had been sitting and talking with Peggy Carley, whom I hadn't seen since 1962 when she went off to marry nice Steve Edelman. They lived in Texas; she was a patent lawyer. We both had grand-children and showed our pictures.

"My grandchildren give me such pleasure," I said. "Particularly my little curly headed grandson, and I get to see him all the time."

Yes, life is still fun, I thought. How can we have been thinking it is over?

I looked out the bay window through the high maple trees of the college grounds and saw three men sauntering up the path to the dorm. One of them, the slight one in the middle, had a familiar loose-limbed gait.

Eagerly I rose from the window seat and went up to the group as they entered the lounge.

"Danny Parker!" I said. "It's you."

The person I had addressed looked toward me. Beneath a somewhat wizened countenance, he exuded an entrenched assurance of boyish charm.

"We heard the classes of the early sixties were in this dorm," Danny said, amid hugs and hellos. "So we came to see who was here." The trio was from the nearby men's college, where their class was also having its reunion.

Paul McKay, sporting a gray ponytail, spoke of remarriage and a two-year-old son.

"That's the age of my grandson," I laughed.

"You're a grandmother," said Danny. "How fantastic."

"And you," I said, "I hear you're a tycoon."

Grandmother, tycoon. It all seemed like make-believe,

the overlay and camouflage of our young true selves. In college Danny had been a charming, wistful drinker. We had been in a play together. One evening he had got me to dance for him in his room, the way you normally dance only for yourself in front of the mirror. I think he was the first person who ever made me feel sexy.

"I'm a mini coon," said Danny.

"Danny's a wonderful family man," said Joe Pearson, the other man. "He's wonderful to his wife and children."

I turned to Joe, a large man with soft brown eyes, whom I vaguely remembered. He had a picture of his younger self around his neck, which, he drew out, slightly abashed, to show me. I looked at a heavyset young man with a low hairline. "Oh yes," I said. I thought, but didn't say, that he looked better now.

"Joe's a calligrapher," said Danny.

"You know what I remember about you?" confided Joe. "Your smile. And you still have it."

Joe and I talked for some time in earnest flirtation, until he was merrily swept off by his friends. After he left, I fingered the piece of paper in my pocket with his address. He lives in Philadelphia but says he often comes to New York.

I like to think it wasn't only the men who cheered me that day. Cheer beamed in the flickering afternoon light of the leaves of the high trees. It lay in the eagerness with which I showed off the pictures of my grandchildren. It resonated in my admiration for Linda Solomon, who has had lupus for a decade and still travels all over the world and copes and does not feel life is over. She and I took a walk before dinner, past familiar and unfamiliar buildings, laughing when we called one building "new" and then realized it had been there for twenty-five years. And the more I thought over the events of the day, the more I rebelled against the mood of our earlier conversation in the circle of women. Not that we had been consciously distorting the state of our lives, but I was sure we were not as sad as we had been representing ourselves. A reunion is an intense and dizzying affair, inviting you, as it foreshortens a lifetime, to feel at once eighteen and eighty. Perhaps our declarations about our mothers, at the end of *their* lives, had been a way of admitting time's awesome power, of talking about our destiny in time as women, bound within our women's bodies. But our ritual regathering at this interval of years also had a more generative aspect. We looked deep into one another's faces and spirits and could see that we were still ourselves, recognizable both within time and despite it. The force of that recognition was palpable. It helped us build the strength we needed to survive our mothers, and then to carry with us their persistent ghosts more joyously and lightly.

When I got back to my home in New York, I sat out in the little square across from my building where a couple of years ago the statue of Eleanor Roosevelt was installed. The Eleanor of the statue is not young, but she doesn't give the sense that age bothers her. Clad in her serviceable coat, leaning on a rock under the pin oaks, she rests her chin on her fist in pensive contemplation and clearly has a lot on her mind. The whole world is still out there. Her capacity to contribute to it is not in doubt. It was my mother who taught me to admire Eleanor Roosevelt, and I heard her speak once in the fifties when I was a girl. She seemed then a formidable figure—a large woman with awesome diction, lecturing from behind a stage podium. The Eleanor under the pin oaks is a softer presence, subtly engaging the onlooker. In one of my reveries I imagine sitting near the statue with my mother, old but sprightly, beside me. We gossip and catch up on things. Eleanor's company puts us in good humor. Then my mother peers at me closely. "Your hair," she hazards, reaching out her hand. "I think it looks very attractive. But if you would just move this one strand . . ."

A Hundred Hearts

"Granny," said Tim, my daughter Sarah's son, "I want to cut you open and put in a hundred hearts." We were walking to my apartment from the nearby playground in Riverside Park. Tim had come to spend the afternoon with me.

"Yes, Tim," I said, hiding my alarm at the suggested surgical incursion.

"So you won't die," he explained. At five Tim is an inventor, a fantasist. In the face of life's intractable conditions, he believes in the power of his schemes.

"And I'll put in energy, so you won't be old," he continued. Tim spoke emphatically, stressing both *energy* and *old*. I wondered if his plan had been worked out in advance.

"And I'll put in happiness," he added. I listened, a little awestruck, delighting in his poetical soul and in his kind-

ness. My life loomed before me. I tried to decide if it needed an infusion of happiness.

"So when I do something bad, you won't be mad at me,"
Tim concluded. The shift in concern from my welfare to
Tim's own jolted me from my swoon of grandmotherly pride.

"Sounds like a good idea, Tim," I said. "But be sure to sew
me up again when you're done."

Tim worries about me growing old and dying. Ever since
I told him that I am too old to chase after him to get him to
put on his socks and shoes, he has brought up my being old
several times. I retort, "I'm not all *that* old," but his concern
persists. Most recently it expressed itself when we were walking along a crowded city street, and, anxious to hang onto
him, I had a firm grip on his hand. Suddenly Tim blurted
out that I had something on my thumb. "No, I don't," I said,
extracting my hand from his and peering at it. "There's
nothing on my thumb." "Yes there is," he insisted. "You have
old on it."

As Tim ponders my decay, I myself feel strangely rejuve-
nated. For one thing, I was the first among my friends to
have a grandchild, and now I have four—Tim here in New
York and Matthew's three in France. Being a grandmother
makes me feel the opposite of old. I'm at the start of something grand and new, and I'm ebullient.

"You're so lucky," say my friends as they go on to complain about the frustrating pace or intentions of their own
grown children.

"I'm sure you'll get your own soon," I console them, but I can't help feeling complacent in my abundance.

It startles me, though, to be envied. I am forced to view myself from the outside, as someone who has what other people want, rather than as the struggling, easily confused person I have always felt myself to be. It startles me, too, because I didn't have a chance to miss having a grandchild. Money or fame yes, I knew their value through my own envy of other people. But here was something that came my way, before I had defined it as one of life's goods and measures.

I have learned to be circumspect, especially with friends who are childless, let alone without grandchildren, or perhaps themselves still trying to have a child. I make it a point not to sound insensitively ecstatic in recounting the latest cute thing Caroline or Tim or Suzanne has said or in reporting, with wry astonishment, that Matthew and his wife have just had their *third* child, Gaston.

"In France that makes them a '*famille nombreuse*,'" I say. "They get free rides on the *métro*." I can tell that my dinner companion, herself now forty-two and about to give up on fertility treatments, is working hard to maintain an even tone in the conversation.

Yes, first out of the gate, I have stayed ahead in the grandmother sweepstakes. When friends my own age began to have their *first* grandchild, there was I working on my fourth. "But *your* children," I learned to counter, "are establishing good professions and earning money. Mine are just blithe breeders." I have worried, genuinely worried, about Sarah's and Matthew's spawning of offspring. There was Sarah, having that baby without a seeming care about marriage or money or even an appropriate mate. "You'll end up taking care of it," my friends said. "She ought not to have it." "She'll have to decide," I said. I have ended up helping Sarah a lot, but the help I give her also helps me. It may be an odd thing to say, but I feel a love for Tim that reminds me of the unconditional way I used to love my dog Tony.

As for Matthew, although he might have seemed more sensible, being married and working, how sensible is it to have three children when you yourself are only twenty-nine and don't know yet what you want to do with your own life? His latest scheme is to move with his family to Ardèche and become a sheepherder. The French government, he tells me, will support this. It seems the French government is as zealous in building up the sheep as it is the human population.

This unexpected stage of my life began with Matthew's call from France. The summer following his college graduation he had gone hiking in Sardinia with the French girlfriend whose name, after Matthew came home from his term abroad, had become familiar to me from the envelopes of her frequent letters. In late August, he phoned from Paris. It wasn't the usual collect call. "Mom," he said, "are you sitting down?"

I wasn't pleased at the news; I wasn't displeased—I didn't

know what to be, just as later I didn't know how to feel
about Sarah. My own first pregnancy had been so much
clearer. I was married; we had jobs. I was twenty-seven.
Even, then, waiting for test results, I had no idea what I
wanted. When the doctor called to say I was pregnant, it surprised me to be so deeply happy.

Matthew explained how he and Marianne had thought a
long time about what to do before deciding finally to go
ahead and have the baby. I tried to keep my tone neutral, all
the time wondering what I was feeling, and indeed what I
should be feeling as a responsible parent. Wasn't he con-
straining his young life? I had imagined his future as a
writer, a photographer, an anthropologist, even a ski bum.
Instead, he'd be changing diapers and worrying about the
rent. The vista seemed dreary. Yet it wasn't only that. A baby.
My son's child. That was thrilling. Matthew told me that he
and Marianne were planning to get married so he could
work in France. "Yes, of course," I said. I was already in my
mind's eye on the plane.

"There's no need for you to come," Matthew said. They
were just going down to the *mairie*.

"You know, I *could* come," I said, trying to sound casual.
"Wouldn't you like your mom there?" Even as I asked, I
knew this was one of those questions you pose at your own
risk.

Matthew tried to be tactful. Since Marianne didn't want
her parents at the ceremony, if his showed up, couldn't I see

the embarrassment? "Come later," he said. "When we have the baby."

The baby was a girl. They named her Caroline. In my life at home it was a sad time for me. My lover had left me for someone else. Even in one's midfifties this can be searing. Nor did it help that I was still smarting from being kicked out of my poker game. "You need to go and hold that child," a friend told me. I didn't know what I needed, but when Matthew sent me a picture of little Caroline bobbing over Marianne's shoulder with a wide-eyed alert little gaze, I got on the phone and booked my ticket for Paris.

Matthew and Marianne were living in a small but neatly appointed apartment in the tenth arrondissement. They had divided the one bedroom into two parts by means of a screen hand painted by Marianne, one part for themselves and the other for the baby. I marveled at such orderliness and attention to aesthetics. Was this my son, whose room at home, so recently, had been strewn with dirty clothes and a clutter of parts of bicycles and of marijuana bongs? As a child, though, he had been neat. I remembered his little shoes aligned carefully at the foot of a chair, on which he had placed his clothes to be worn the next day. In such quotidian details can be read someone's future and his soul.

When Matthew and Marianne went out to their jobs, I had my first time alone with the baby. She was sleeping when they left, but after she awoke, I lifted her from her crib and carried her, my hand cupping her head, over to Matthew and Marianne's bed. Lying down, I put her on my stomach, and for a long time I watched her bob her head and grope with her little hands. I used to lie like this with my own children, but then, of course, I had milk for them. I remembered the way their heads and mouths and fingers moved toward my breasts. Caroline had no interest in my breasts. There was nothing there for her. In any case, she was being bottle-fed. Marianne hadn't wanted to nurse. I got up after a while and prepared the baby's formula. After I had fed and changed her, I put her in her pram and set out for the Place des Vosges, pushing her along with a sense of our escapade, looking down at my little bright-eyed co-conspirator. In the elegant Place, we found a nice spot under a tree. Young girls came up to us. *O qu'elle est mignonne; qu'elle a l'air intelligent.* "*Oui*," I said, "*Je suis la grandmère. De l'Amèrique. Je suis venue de New York pour la voir.*" I let them hold the baby, wondering if Matthew and Marianne would approve.

Marianne was difficult to talk to, and I couldn't quite blame it on my French or her English. She was reserved. I sensed that she didn't particularly like me. "She thinks you're judging her," said Matthew. "Me judging her!" I exclaimed. "Isn't it the other way round?"

Matthew was the overt judge, criticizing even my way of washing the dishes. I had been doing my best in the small, unfamiliar kitchen when he came in to watch me. "Are you squirting the detergent directly onto the dishes?" he asked.

"Why yes. Isn't that all right?"

"Well, I know detergent's not that expensive. So why make a big deal of it? But look," he said, guiding me out of the way and taking my place, "if you squirt the detergent on the sponge, it lasts ten times longer."

I watched him, incredulously, admiringly.

"See," he said, a few minutes later. "I'm on my tenth dish and the sponge is still soapy."

That task completed, we drifted back into the living room where Marianne was giving the baby her bottle. "*Écoute*," said Matthew to his wife, "*tu veux savoir comment elle fait la vaisselle?*"—do you want to know how she does the dishes?

But it was Matthew who suggested we march in Gay Pride March, the annual event that sets its route from Montparnasse to Bastille. "Do you really want to?" I asked, intrigued but doubtful of his motives. "What could be your interest?"

"Oh I can take photographs," he said. "I think it could be fun."

So Matthew packed Caroline into her pram, and he and I and his baby—three generations of our family—headed to the *métro*. I admired the way he lifted the pram down and up the stairs. Youth. Manhood. Domesticity. I remembered the good early days of my own marriage.

Getting out at Montparnasse, we joined the crowd of what seemed largely young homosexual men, a good number of them in drag, and a smaller number of women, on the whole older and less flamboyant. It was a balmy late June day. We marched along, Matthew asking me to push the pram so he could be free to take photos. Men and women with shaven heads, tattoos, and leather marched past us; antic transvestites in gaudy wigs, boots, and dresses looked into the pram; lesbian couples in work shirts and jeans— West Village types, I might have said—held hands and looked at one another. Matthew photographed the transvestites, and the transvestites photographed Caroline. I think she was the only baby in the parade, looking up from her pram with her alert, expressive little face. "*Je suis la grand-mère*," I repeated to onlookers. A French TV reporter, a woman, came up to me.

"What are you doing here?" she asked.

"Well, if I were in New York, I'm not sure I'd be marching. But here it seemed the thing to do."

"So you'd be ashamed to march in New York?" she insinuated.

"I'm not saying that," I said.

"What are you saying?" She was persistent.

"I'm saying I support the march, and I am here with my son and granddaughter."

"Phew," I thought as she walked away. I looked at Caroline, beaming from the pram. What a great thing to do. The different parts of my life—my son, the baby, my love for women—all seemed to be coming together in this strange and marvelous way. A passing transvestite in a beehive black wig swooped by Caroline's pram. "*Ah, le plus jeune!*" he exclaimed.

"What did the reporter want?" asked Matthew, coming back to my side.

"She wanted to know what I'm doing here."

"And what *are* you doing here?" Matthew probed.

I paused to find a good answer.

"Perhaps it's enough," I said, "that you and I wanted to do this." I reached up to pat his shoulder, and we moved along with the crowd.

At my house on Long Island, Tim and I have been drawing pictures and writing letters as our rainy afternoon activities. One letter has been drafted for his cousins, Caroline, Suzanne, and Gaston, who came to visit in the summer. Tim learned to ask Caroline to play with him. "*Veux-tu jouer avec moi?*" And she said back to him, "Okay!" I have visions of them visiting back and forth when they are older. Maybe Caroline will come to college in America. Of course, Tim will speak perfect French.

Tim also has drawn a picture of a fire truck. "What else should I put in?" he asked me as he worked on its final embellishments. "A ladder," I suggested. "A hose."

"I've got those," he said.

"Well, the firefighters," I said.

"That's too hard," he said. "What else?"

"You could put in a dog," I said. "A Dalmatian. That's the kind of dog, white with black spots, that rides on fire trucks."

"You do it," he said. And I did.

Now we're getting ready for the evening. Tim is in his pajamas, but he's being allowed to stay up for a while. My friends arrive, a group of women—my Long Island group—who'll be playing poker with me for a stretch of hours. I am putting the snacks and drinks out on a counter, and one friend, seated at the table, is setting up the game.

"Come over here," she beckons to Tim, who moves trustingly to her side. "How would you like to help me count out the chips?" She puts her arm lightly around him.

Tim nods and gets to work. Soon in front of him is a line of little stacks—four white chips to each stack. He explains to me, as if I didn't know it, that the stacks need to be all the same size.

"Oops," he says, confident that without him we would blunder. "This pile needs one more chip." Tim rectifies the error.

"Granny," he says, looking up at me. "Now you can play your game."

ABOUT THE AUTHOR

Wendy Fairey is the author of *One of the Family* (Norton, 1992), a memoir of growing up in Hollywood as the daughter of gossip columnist Sheilah Graham and discovering the identity of her true father, the British philosopher A. J. Ayer. She holds a doctorate from Columbia University in English and comparative literature and teaches English literature and creative writing at Brooklyn College in New York. She lives in New York City and East Hampton, Long Island, and has two children and four grandchildren.